From *The Black Paw*

Dinner was served in almost total silence. They were all there: Hattie and Franny, Ross and Allan, but they had nothing to say to each other even when Mr. Keith and I were out of the room.

At the conclusion of the meal Ross stood up and announced that he could not stand the house any longer and was going to drive to the nearest large town and find something to do. Hattie immediately showed signs of animation and said she'd go, too, but Ross shook his head and explained that he wasn't going anywhere where she could properly accompany him. Hattie's eyes were hard, and she turned to me and told me to send Oliver to her. I delivered this message, and Oliver took time to scowl blackly before he went in to her.

Hattie told him to bring the car around, as she was going to the movies. She carefully iced the order before giving it, and I decided that she and Oliver must have had a quarrel.

Franny spoke up at this point and gave it as her opinion that Hattie ought to stay at home and attend to her mourning. To be seen at the movies under the circumstances, Franny observed, was in very low taste. Hattie did not take the trouble even to answer.

Allan ignored them all completely, and I knew he was quite drunk.

Jennie and I cleared up, as usual, and I decided that if you were going to be a servant it was much better to be a male servant.

I put this view before Jennie, but she merely observed that if God had made you a female in the first place, you couldn't possibly hope to be a male servant.

I went straight upstairs after we had finished, and as I approached my room I heard the swish and creak of the rocking chair. I groaned inwardly and resigned myself to being stuck with Franny again.

But it was not Franny in my rocking chair; it was no one at all. And the empty chair, still swaying a little, eased to a stop as I stood there watching it

Books by Constance & Gwenyth Little

The Grey Mist Murders (1938)
The Black-Headed Pins (1938)
The Black Gloves (1939)
Black Corridors (1940)
The Black Paw (1941)
The Black Shrouds (1941)
The Black Thumb (1942)
The Black Rustle (1943)
The Black Honeymoon (1944)
Great Black Kanba (1944)
The Black Eye (1945)
The Black Stocking (1946)
The Black Goatee (1947)
The Black Coat (1948)
The Black Piano (1948)
The Black Smith (1950)
The Black House (1950)
The Blackout (1951)
The Black Dream (1952)
The Black Curl (1953)
The Black Iris (1953)

The Black Paw

By Constance & Gwenyth Little

The Rue Morgue Press
Boulder, Colorado

The Black Paw
Copyright © 1941, 1967.
Reprinted with the permission of
the authors' estate.

New material copyright © 2001
by The Rue Morgue Press

ISBN: 0-915230-37-2

Any resemblance to persons living or dead
would be downright ridiculous.

Printed at Johnson Printing
Boulder, Colorado

The Rue Morgue Press
P.O. Box 4119
Boulder, CO 80306

PRINTED IN THE UNITED STATES OF AMERICA

About the Littles

Although all but one of their books had "black" in the title, the 21 mysteries of Constance (1899-1980) and Gwenyth (1903-1985) Little were far from somber affairs. The two Australian-born sisters from East Orange, New Jersey, were far more interested in coaxing chuckles than in inducing chills from their readers.

Indeed, after their first book, *The Grey Mist Murders*, appeared in 1938, Constance rebuked an interviewer for suggesting that their murders weren't realistic by saying, "Our murderers strangle. We have no sliced-up corpses in our books." However, as the books mounted, the Littles did go in for all sorts of gruesome murder methods—"horrible," was the way their own mother described them—which included the occasional sliced-up corpse.

But the murders were always off stage and tempered by comic scenes in which bodies and other objects, including swimming pools, were constantly disappearing and reappearing. The action took place in large old mansions, boarding houses, hospitals, hotels, or on trains or ocean liners, anywhere the Littles could gather together a large cast of eccentric characters, many of whom seemed to have escaped from a Kaufman play or a Capra movie. The typical Little heroine—each book was a stand-alone—often fell under suspicion herself and turned detective to keep the police from slapping the cuffs on. Whether she was a working woman or a spoiled little rich brat, she always spoke her mind, kept her sense of humor, and got her man, both murderer and husband. But if marriage was in the offing, it was always on her terms and the vows were taken with more than a touch of cynicism. Love was grand, but it was even grander if the husband could either pitch in with the cooking and cleaning or was wealthy enough to hire household help.

The Littles wrote all their books in bed—"Chairs give one backaches," Gwenyth complained—with Constance providing detailed plot outlines while Gwenyth did the final drafts. Over the years that pattern changed somewhat but Constance always insisted that Gwen "not mess up my clues." Those clues were everywhere and the Littles made sure there were no loose ends. Seemingly irrelevant events were revealed to be of major significance in the final summation.

The Littles published their two final novels, *The Black Curl* and *The Black Iris*, in 1953, and if they missed writing after that, they were at least able to devote more time to their real passion—traveling. The two made at least three trips around the world at a time when that would have been a major expedition. For more information on the Littles and their books, see the introductions by Tom & Enid Schantz to The Rue Morgue Press editions of *The Black Glove*s and *The Black Honeymoon.*

CHAPTER ONE

When Selma Barton first came to me with the craziest of all her crazy ideas, it had started to rain. It was a Saturday, the thirteenth of May, a gray, chilly day that made my spring clothes look silly—and it continued to rain, on and off, for a solid week—as though in sorrow at anyone being stupid enough to take one of Selma's ideas seriously.

I happened to see her from my window as she stepped out of a taxi at the hotel entrance, and as I watched her cross the pavement and disappear inside I knew, somehow, that she was brewing something and wanted my help.

I turned away from the window and worried quietly for a few minutes. Selma's ideas were of the type that issue from cracked pots, and under ordinary circumstances I would not have bothered even to listen to her. But she had me on a spot.

I was going places with a handsome actor—a smooth specimen who had been married to three rich women at different times and divorced again by each and every one. My parents were seriously opposed to my even seeing him. They were not wealthy, but they pointed out to me that they were anxious to hang onto the bit they had. It was a reasonable attitude, and yet I could not bring myself to obey them. The man was too handsome, and besides, all my girlfriends envied me.

Selma, with a bit of judicious lying here and there, had made it easy for me to see him—but she had my fate in her hands. She had only to tell my parents the truth, and I'd be whisked away to Kansas, or somewhere, since they couldn't afford Honolulu.

So I continued to worry until Selma burst into my room, when I became actively alarmed. She was positively quivering.

"Callie!" she said dramatically. "You must help me."

She helped herself to a cigarette and waved it about excitedly as she talked.

The plan was simple enough—and worse than anything I had imagined. I knew that her marriage had just gone on the rocks and that she was preparing to get a divorce, but she told me now that her husband was unfortunately in possession of what she called the whip hand, and he was directing the proceedings—including the amount of alimony. "And it isn't enough, Callie. I absolutely must have more."

"Why don't you tell him that?" I asked warily.

"Don't be feeble. I have, of course. But he won't budge."

"The whip hand?"

"Yes, and that's what I want to talk to you about."

It all boiled down to the fact that Selma had sent out a couple of love letters that had somehow fallen into the hands of this cold-blooded monster—her husband—and he had threatened to show them to the world at large if she did not obey instructions. "And I couldn't face that," she said pathetically. "People would be shocked. Although, as a matter of fact, I only meant them in fun."

She mashed her cigarette in an ashtray and left it still smoking, as usual. I watched her while she removed her newest spring hat and stepped over to a mirror to titivate. She was very handsome, built on showgirl proportions and with absolutely genuine-looking blonde hair.

"And so?" I prodded uneasily.

It seemed that she had to get those letters somehow, and only this morning fate had shown her the way. She had seen an advertisement in the paper for a housemaid in the Barton menage, and I was to secure the job, steal the letters and bring them to her.

I laughed. "Listen," I said, "I was brought up soft. I've never had to do any hard work, and I don't think it would agree with me."

"There's nothing hard about it," she protested. "You just do bits of housework. You go about in a pretty costume with a feather duster—that's all. And the minute you get those letters you can leave. In fact, you'd better. You won't have to stay more than two days at the outside, because I think I know where he keeps them." She paused for a moment and added, "It's really a life-and-death matter, Callie, and I've done a lot for you, you know."

"I work with a feather duster and a pretty uniform in the daytime—and with a pretty negligee at night," I said musingly. "Sounds like adventure, anyway. When am I supposed to sleep?"

She passed that over and said brightly, "You can get the job—easily. You've only to say you're Scotch; they like Scotch help. They have a sort of cook-and-butler combination who have been there for years and years—Jennie and Wallace Keith—and they're Scotch. And of course you'd look Scotch, too, with your black hair and blue eyes."

"I thought that was Irish," I said coldly.

"Oh no—no, indeed, Scotch. And your lovely complexion, too—the creamy, satiny texture of your skin."

I said, "Wait a minute, Selma. Don't let's waste time while you try to do this the nice way. Just tell me in a few terse words what you are planning in case I refuse."

She took another cigarette, crossed her legs and sighed. "I hate to be mean, Callie, but I must have those letters before the divorce comes up. If you refuse me I'll have to tell your parents, frankly, that I think they should know that their daughter is caught fast in a quicksand of infatuation and deception, and—"

"Cease," I said wearily. "Tell me exactly what I'm supposed to do, and keep the long words like quicksand and infatuation out of it."

Selma appeared to relax a little. "It's simple," she said cheerfully. "You just phone up and say your name is Ellen McTavish."

"Ellen—what?" I asked, astounded.

"McTavish. Scotch, you see. And I have a couple of very fine references for you."

"Wait a minute," I said feverishly. "You say you know where those letters are kept?"

"Yes, certainly. I expect it will be just an overnight job."

"And if I'm caught?"

"I'll come forward at once," she declared heroically. "Allan won't prosecute you, or anything. He's not the type. He's very gallant, really."

"Why did you leave him then?" I asked, not really caring.

"As a matter of fact, I didn't want to leave—if you must know. He told me to go and get a divorce."

"Why didn't you refuse?"

"I did," Selma explained simply, "but he pointed out to me that I'd be better off living an independent life, with an allowance from him, than merely boarding in his house with no allowance. So I left."

"Of course," I murmured.

"Now, listen," said Selma firmly, "if you bring me those letters I'll give you my roadster."

That clinched it, of course. I wanted the roadster desperately; it was a beauty and not much use to Selma, as she couldn't drive.

We telephoned to the Barton house without further discussion, and to my horror I was engaged on the spot, without having to show my face. I was told that I would be expected on the following day at four-thirty in the afternoon. I didn't catch the name of the place, and I was too numb to ask for a repetition, but Selma said it didn't matter, because she'd put me on the train herself and give me all directions. "I'll go right go over to Hoboken with you," she declared handsomely.

"Hoboken!" I whispered in a hollow voice.

"It's all right. You won't see anything of Hoboken; you merely take a train there. Now let's go out, and I'll buy you the prettiest uniform in town."

"What about the feather duster?"

"Oh, they'll supply that," she said carelessly.

Rain was still dripping dismally the next morning when Selma called for me. I was arrayed splendidly in sports apparel and had three large suitcases and a hatbox—and my parents stood in the background with beaming faces.

I was supposed to be going to the country home of Selma's prize-exhibit friends—the Smith-Hartwells. They had everything of which Mother approved, and I could see that she thought I was on the right road at last.

We had to stop at Selma's apartment so that I could shed my luggage and pick up a small suitcase containing the uniform and a few toilet accessories. We had quite a fuss about the clothes I was wearing. I wanted to continue wearing them, but Selma declared that it would be absurd. She insisted that I put on an old raincoat she had and an even older black felt hat. "You must look like a maid," she reasoned. "You couldn't walk in with that coat on you; they'd think you'd stolen it and bounce you before you ever got the job—or the letters."

"I don't see why," I protested, jabbing my arms viciously into the raincoat. "From the data I have collected at ladies' luncheons I should say that maids have more money to spend on clothes than anyone else."

"Nevertheless," said Selma firmly, "you are wearing the raincoat and the black felt."

I was so nervous by the time we got to Hoboken that I believe I'd have gone straight home and faced the consequences if I'd had time to think about it. But there was a train leaving within a few minutes, and Selma bought a ticket, bundled me onto it and gave me the names of my station and the two preceding stations. Just before she left me she threw over her shoulder that if there was no conveyance at the station I was to walk along the road until I came to a yellow brick wall with a pair of iron gates at which I turned in.

She disappeared then, and I had a moment of panic. A yellow brick wall and iron gates had a gloomy and isolated sound, somehow.

The train began to move, and I settled back into my seat and stonily ignored Selma, who was waving to me from the platform. I wrote down the names of the two stations preceding mine, opened a box of candy and prepared to wait.

I waited two hours.

I was in such a temper when at last I arrived that I would have taken the first train back had there been one. But the station was a small shed, tightly locked up and showing no signs of life. I was the only passenger to get off there, and there was no conveyance of any sort.

It was raining harder than ever, and I watched the train disappear with mixed feelings of desolation and fury at Selma for glossing over the hardships she must have known were facing me.

I glanced around at the scenery, which seemed to consist of trees, rain and one lone road. There was not a living soul in sight anywhere, and I was chilled and hungry. I hesitated—put a mental conjure on Selma and hoped that it would work—and then tackled the road.

I must have walked for at least half an hour before the yellow wall came into view, and the wall went on for five minutes before I hit the gate. I was soaked through and through, and I jerked Selma's old felt hat off my head and threw it furiously away into the shrubbery.

The house was of brick, square and ugly, huddled into itself and sprouting to a height of four stories, as though there were not plenty of ground around it into which it might have spread.

I stood still in the rain, looking at it for a while, hating to go in. It was just getting dark, and there was a light in one of the downstairs rooms, but the other windows were blank and looked bleak and cheerless. There was no sound but the cold drip of rain on wet leaves.

My hair was plastered to my forehead, and small rivulets were wandering lazily down my neck. I took a step forward, and at the same time a faint sound drew my eyes upward.

One of the windows just under the roof on the fourth floor had been raised. As I stared, a woman leaned far out and, without a downward glance, raised her arms and appeared to be feeling around the roof with her hands.

CHAPTER TWO

I STARED through the sodden dusk and wondered what on earth the woman could be doing. It was too dark to see her clearly. I could tell that she was wearing something of a lightish color, and that was about all.

I watched her until she suddenly backed in. The show seemed to be over then, so I shrugged and moved along to the front door.

I pressed a finger on the bell and then remembered that I should probably have gone around to the back. I didn't much care by that time, though—I was very hungry, wet through and completely disgusted with Selma and all her works.

The door was presently jerked open by a man who looked as irritable as I felt. He was tall and dark, with rather fierce-looking black eyes, and I knew that he must be either Selma's ex or the chauffeur, because, according to the list of house occupants she had given me, they were the only good-looking men on the place.

He frowned at me and was obviously about to say, "We don't want any," when I stepped in quickly. "I'm the new housemaid," I said and sneezed violently.

He gave me a brief running over with his eyes and then closed the door behind me. "Franny!" he called abruptly.

There was no reply, and I glanced down self-consciously at the lake that was slowly welling around me on the oriental rug.

The man stepped to the foot of the high, narrow staircase and called again, more sharply: "Franny! Come down here, will you?"

A swishing from above accompanied a pair of feet which presently bore an elderly woman into view. She was so thin that her pale blue dress looked as though it were on a hanger. Her face was lined and sallow, and her gray hair untidy and badly arranged. I mentally consulted Selma's list and placed her as "Frances Barton, spinster—Allan's old-pill half sister."

She called, "What is it, Allan?" and he said briefly, "New housemaid's here."

She came down the last few stairs and gave me a sharp look. "You're late. It's after six."

I was wondering if it was she I had seen at the window, and I said rather absently, "I'm sorry, Miss Barton; it was the train. It took so long to get here."

Allan gave me a penetrating look, and I had an uncomfortable feeling that I had not spoken as Ellen McTavish should.

He turned to his sister and said, "Don't be silly, Franny. You can't expect anyone to get to a place like this exactly on time." He glanced, at me again. "Did you walk from the station?"

I tried to put a bit more of Ellen into it this time. "Yes sir, and a rare nice walk, too, sir. It was raining a treat."

Franny clicked her tongue; Allan looked at me in silence, and I looked at the lake on the rug.

After a moment Allan said crisply, "Why wasn't she met at the station?"

"My dear brother, we cannot be sending the servants around in cars. Absurd!"

"It's a good deal more absurd—not to mention the expense of the thing—to let a girl walk two miles through the rain when Oliver and the car are doing nothing!" He turned to me. "What's your name?"

I nearly said: "Callie Drake," and bit it back just in time. "Ellen McTavish, sir."

He gave me an odd look and repeated the name after me. "All right, Ellen. Tomorrow you are to go into the village and buy yourself a new dress and a new pair of shoes. You will accompany Miss Barton when she goes in to do her marketing, and she will charge the things to my account."

He turned away abruptly and disappeared into a room on the left, and Franny was free to show extreme annoyance, which she promptly did.

She muttered, "Ridiculous! Quite absurd!" several times, and then she caught sight of the lake.

She loosed a young scream, flopped down onto her knees and began to mop at it with her hands. I pulled out my handkerchief and wiped it up for her.

"If Madam would be kind enough to show me my room," I suggested, "I'd like to take off my wet things."

She said, "Yes, of course, certainly. Follow me," and started up the stairs. She added an inquiry as to why I had come to the front door instead of going around to the back.

I told her I had lost my way in the garden and had somehow mixed front and rear. I added an apology and an assurance that in all my fifteen years of service I had never made such a bad break before.

The stairway was steep and went straight up without any bends or curves. The second flight, leading to the third floor, was built directly above the first flight, and the third directly above the second. It transpired, rather to my surprise, that my room was on the third floor. I had imagined a retreat under the eaves on the top story. It was small, with bits and pieces of old-fashioned furniture obviously discarded from the rest of the house.

Franny patted the bed, rearranged an alarm clock on the bureau and prepared to withdraw.

"What is the fourth floor used for?" I asked suddenly.

She frowned reprovingly. "You mustn't start being inquisitive, Ellen. We don't use it or anything but storage space. Now come down to the kitchen as soon as you've changed your clothes. We're waiting for our supper."

She went out and closed the door, and I muttered wildly, "Supper!" I had lived all my life in hotels, and while I supposed I could handle a feather duster, I knew nothing whatever about preparing a meal.

I sighed and unpacked my overnight bag. After all, I'd be leaving in the morning. I was quite determined that nothing would keep me there any longer. I'd get the letters that night and Selma's roadster the following afternoon.

I was so thoroughly soaked that I had to change into the other set of underwear I'd brought. The only other dress I had was the uniform, so I removed the price tags and slipped it on. It was vastly becoming—a shimmering gray silk, with a lace cap and tiny lace-trimmed apron. I admired myself in the mirror for a while, and then I glanced down at my shoes. They were sodden and dark with water, and I had no others. I could not walk around in shoes that squished with every step, and for a moment I considered going down in my stockinged feet, and then my eyes fell on the bedroom slippers I had brought.

They would have to do, of course. I slipped into them, and was conscious of a vague regret that I had not brought something a bit quieter. They were bright red satin, with high slim rhinestone heels and rhinestone buckles on the vamps.

I found the bathroom was right next to my own room. It was immense, with linoleum-covered floor and the largest bathtub I had ever seen, standing on four claw legs. In addition to the old-fashioned plumbing, there were two chairs, a table, a wardrobe and a fancy calendar hanging on the wall. Someone had penciled a ring around May fourteenth.

"That's today," I thought. "If it was a birthday I hope they remembered."

I went on down the stairs and landed myself in the front hall again. I was standing there, wondering how to get to the kitchen, when a man came out from one of the rooms. He was elderly and bald, and there was a resemblance to Franny. I placed him as Allan's half brother, George.

He caught sight of me, stopped dead in his advance and backed up against the wall. "God bless my soul!" he muttered, and it sounded more like piety than expletive.

"I'm the new maid," I explained hastily. "Ellen McTavish, sir. Would you direct me to the kitchen, please?"

He kept his eyes on me for a moment, with a sort of rabbitlike fascination, and then he said feebly, "The kitchen. Yes—yes, of course."

He led the way down a long dark corridor that ran behind the stairs and eventually brought us to another flight of stairs, steeper and narrower than the first. I realized, with a faint sigh, that these were the back stairs, and I should have used them.

The corridor ended in a door which gave on to a square, dark foyer. It had doors on its four side—the one we had just come through—two, half open, on each side, and one straight ahead. Those on the sides apparently led one to the cellar and the other into a washroom. The one in front of us opened to reveal a kitchen of vast and immaculate proportions.

Franny was perched on a stool at a table in the center, looking thoroughly annoyed. She raised her head as I came in, and I could see reproof give way to simple astonishment. Her jaw dropped open.

I paused and felt more uncomfortably overdressed than I ever had in my life.

Franny regained control of her jaw and said shrilly, "Mercy, girl! What in the living world is that you're wearing?"

"Well—I—my trunks haven't come—and this is all I brought with me. I usually reserve it for—for teas and things."

She nodded. "I see. Yes. Well, it's much too outlandish for any occasion in my home. Now when your other things come you are to take it off, and you're not to wear it here again."

"No ma'am," I said cheerfully.

She began to give me rapid directions about the preparation of supper, and as soon as I could push a word in I said firmly, "I'm very sorry, madam, but my training has been in dusting and—and things, and I know nothing whatever about cooking."

She was thoroughly put out, and she said so without reservation. "Do you mean to tell me," she finished up, "that you cannot prepare the simple meal I have outlined?"

"If you'll tell me what to do," I suggested, "I shall be very willing to learn."

That seemed to hit the right spot, and she actually smiled. She began to rattle around the kitchen, pouring out instructions to me in a steady stream, while I trailed around after her helplessly.

She presently said something to me about omelets and sent me into the pantry for some eggs. It was a huge place, neat and cool and with a faint, pleasant smell of coffee. There was a large calendar tacked onto the wall, and May fourteenth had been circled in pencil.

I could not find the eggs, and Franny presently burst in behind me in a fury. She located them at once in a place I had not thought of looking and immediately sent me to the dining room to lay the table.

I felt that this was a job I could really do at last, and I put my soul into it. When I had finished I felt bound to stand and admire it for a while—it looked so pretty.

Franny banged through the swinging door with a shrill question as to why I was taking so long and never waited for an answer. Her eyes fell on the table, and she gave an outraged little shriek.

"Mercy, heavens, girl! You've used my grandmother's china and the sterling silver. Never touch those things. We use them Thanksgiving and Christmas, and Keith is the only one who handles them."

She rushed back into the kitchen, and I rushed after her. Things were going at a furious pace by now. Several pots were bubbling on the stove, and Franny looked due to go off her head at any minute. She fired instructions, commands and reproofs at me, and I stumbled around trying to do what I was told.

Rather suddenly, it seemed to me, the peak of the confusion passed and the pace began to slow down. I even had time after a while to get myself a glass of water at the sink. I noticed that there was another calendar over the sink, and again the fourteenth of May had been circled.

I glanced at Franny who was vigorously slicing bread and asked, "Is it somebody's birthday today, Miss Barton? I've noticed that all the calendars have today's date marked on them."

Franny raised her head and stared, first at me and then at the calendar. She made no reply to my question, and in the little silence that followed she slid quietly to the floor in a dead faint.

CHAPTER THREE

I LOOKED at her helplessly for a moment. Her face was ghastly, and I could not tell whether she was breathing or not.

I called, "Help," rather feebly and then tried to lift her legs up. It didn't appear to benefit her, so I dropped them again and ran into the dining room. I yelled, "Help" again, and much louder, and then I raced back to the kitchen. I filled a glass at the sink and threw the water into her face.

Allan and George Barton appeared just then, and Allan lifted her from the floor and carried her through the dining room to a living room beyond. He put her onto a couch, and he and George went to work on her. I thought that they did not seem much concerned.

She began to come out of it after a while, and Allan left George to it and turned to me.

"Miss Barton is subject to fainting spells," he explained. "She'll be all right now. What was she doing in the kitchen?"

"She was flying around and working her head off, telling me how to get supper," I said, forgetting I was Ellen.

He frowned and said irritably, "Four servants, and Franny must be working in the kitchen." He turned to George. "Where's Oliver?"

"Hattie says he's visiting a sick relative."

Allan said, "Damn his sick relatives. When he wants an extra day off hereafter, he's to come to me about it."

"It's nothing to do with me," George said huffily. "You'd better tell the women."

Allan, still frowning, turned back to me and apparently noticed my costume for the first time. He looked at me for an astonished moment and then barked, "For God's sake, girl, what is it? Something left over from the Follies?"

I felt myself blushing, as I hastily explained about the slippers, and added that the costume was really for when Madam served tea.

"Madam doesn't serve tea," he said shortly. "Get the supper onto the table and ring the bell in the dining room when it's ready."

I went back to the kitchen and spent a frantic five minutes getting the contents of the pots into dishes and thence to the dining-room table. I hoped they were all properly cooked, but I had no way of knowing, so I rang the bell and waited.

I had arranged four places at the table, according to Franny's instructions, but George was the only one who appeared in answer to the bell. He seated himself and appeared to go into a trance. I wondered vaguely what I was supposed to do next.

Allan presently came in, and George stirred, picked up his napkin and laid it on his knee.

Allan sat down and asked abruptly, "Where's Hattie?" I remembered that Hattie was George's wife.

"Sick headache," George said briefly. "She wants to be left alone." He cleared his throat and proceeded to say grace, while I watched him with my mouth hanging slightly open.

They began to help themselves from the various dishes, and I nearly bit off one of my highly polished nails, wondering what my next move was.

Allan put me out of my misery at last. He glanced at me and said, "We'll ring if we want you, Ellen," and I escaped to the kitchen on a long breath of relief.

I partially relieved my hunger with various bits of scraps and devoutly hoped that they'd leave some of what was in the dining room.

A bell rang suddenly above my head, and I jumped and hurried into the dining room. Both men looked up with obvious inquiry, and I stammered, "Did you ring?"

"No," said George Barton.

I returned to the kitchen, and the bell rang again.

It occurred to me suddenly that it might be the front door, so I wended my way through the long, dark corridor to the entrance hall. I had a brief struggle with the heavy door, but at last I swung it open.

A man stepped in and dropped a wet suitcase onto the oriental rug. He was young, tall and good-looking, and after a quick mental checkup I knew that he was not on Selma's list.

He removed his dripping hat and top coat and flung them onto a chair, and then he looked at me and gave a long low whistle.

"I'm the new housemaid, sir. Ellen McTavish."

"You're a sight for sore eyes," he said and laughed. He added, "Selma's jazzing the old place up a bit."

So he knew Selma, but apparently he had not heard of the divorce. I supposed he might be one of her friends.

"Family in?" he asked.

"In the dining room, sir. Whom shall I announce?"

"Don't you bother, sugar. I'll announce myself."

He started down the corridor and opened a door on the left, which turned out to be another entrance into the dining room. He did not close it behind him, and I lingered outside with my ears stretched.

Allan gave him a hearty welcome, and George said rather primly, "How do you do, Ross?"

"Had your dinner?" Allan asked. Ross must have said no, because he added, "Sit down then. Both the women are hors de combat."

"Both?" Ross's voice repeated in some surprise. "Thought there were three in all."

"Selma's cleared out," Allan explained with unmistakable cheerfulness. "She's living in the big city, brewing a divorce."

"Well, well—you never know, do you?" Ross said, apparently without embarrassment. "Here today and gone tomorrow."

"Disgraceful thing!" George's voice boomed suddenly. "Utterly disgraceful. 'Those whom God hath joined together—' "

"Trend of the times, old boy," Allan's voice observed with a faint amusement. "You shouldn't take it so hard."

"But she had everything," Ross said, "including the right curves in the right places. Give me her address, will you, Allan? If you have it, that is."

"I'll write it down for you. You might like to marry her after the divorce. She was a lot of fun."

A chair was pushed back abruptly, and I saw George stalk into the living room beyond with outrage in every line of his figure.

I went back to the kitchen and waited until the other two had finished. What they had left was cold, and there was not much of it, but I ate it hungrily and then climbed the back stairs to my room.

Selma had given me two places in which to look for the letters. One was in a small study on the first floor, and the other was in Allan's bedroom. The bedroom, of course, I'd have to tackle in the morning while I was feather-dusting it, but I figured on the study that night after everyone had gone to bed.

I glanced down at my wrist and then remembered, with a spasm of annoyance, that Selma had made me remove my watch and leave it with her. The alarm clock on the bureau was not going, so I wound it and set it at eleven o'clock. It was a bad guess, as it turned out. It must have been about a quarter past nine at that time.

I stretched out on my bed and waited until the battered old alarm clock stood at twelve-thirty. I decided they'd all be in bed by then, so I crept out and went quietly down the back stairs. I had made up my mind to go to the kitchen first and proceed with due caution from there.

As far as I could see the first floor was dark, except for a light in the kitchen, and I remembered having left that on myself.

I walked into the kitchen and was badly shocked to find a man standing there. He appeared to be in his late forties, tall and thin and a little stooped, with sparse, sandy-colored hair.

He looked me over and then raised his voice and called, "Jennie."

A stout woman with dark hair and small, pale eyes emerged from the pantry. She looked at me, too, and the eyes widened. "Mercy on us! Are you the new maid?"

I nodded.

"You're much too fancy for this house, my girl."

I glanced at the man, who was fingering a heavy gold watch chain that lay across his vest. He dropped his eyes, and I said flippantly, "Fancy is as fancy does."

"That's just it," the woman said grimly. "What makes you think you can run up to your room and leave dishes and food lying all over the place after a meal?"

The dishes! It had never entered my head to wash them before I left. I was about to snap back a reply, when I gave it a second thought. It would be better not to make an enemy of her, and in any case, I could hardly blame her for being in a temper. It must have been a bit disheartening to return from her day off and find all that mess lying around.

She hung up a damp dishcloth and observed bitterly, "Mr. Keith and I have been clearing up here for the last hour."

I suppressed a smile at the "Mr. Keith" part of it and said contritely, "I'm awfully sorry, really. I just came down to do it myself. You see, I felt quite ill after dinner, and I had to lie down—but I'm much better now."

"What's your name?" she asked curtly, her small eyes still cloudy with suspicion.

"Ellen McTavish."

"Oh well." It seemed to fix everything, for she started a long discussion about Scotland, and even the silent Mr. Keith was inspired to put in an occasional word.

I have never been to Scotland, but it presently transpired that I had come from Edinburgh, while they hailed from Glasgow. Only the way they pronounced it, it sounded like Glazgy. I had spent my tender years in an orphanage, and they both came from large families. We had all come to the United States for the same reason—the higher wages.

We were quite pally by the time we got upstairs. Their room was across the hall from mine, and they said good night to me at my door. I went into my room and set my clock correctly at twenty minutes past eleven.

I undressed this time and slipped into my robe. I felt that it was a bit early for nocturnal intrigue, but I simply could not wait any longer.

I crept down the stairs again, hating it every inch of the way. It was pitch dark, and the silence sang in my ears.

I reached the first floor and discovered that light was glowing from the half-opened door leading to the dining room. I held my breath, went softly down the corridor and cautiously peered in.

George Barton was seated at the cleared table, and on it, directly in front of him, lay his watch.

CHAPTER FOUR

I STARED at him, first with surprise, and then with growing impatience. He just sat there, drumming his fingers on the table, and I felt that Selma had probably been right in her opinion that George and Franny were both cracked.

I waited for a moment and then decided to go and search for the letters, anyway. According to Selma, the small study was over on the other side of the house, and George looked as though he might be a fixture in the dining room for a while.

I went quietly along the dark corridor to the black darkness of the front hall, where I had to grope for the sliding doors that opened into the drawing room. The study was at the end of the drawing room, and there was no other entrance to it.

I worked the sliding doors apart with the utmost care, but just as I had them wide enough so that I could slip through, they let out a metallic squeak. I froze into immobility, and I don't think I even breathed for a while. But George did not appear, and the silence was broken only by the tapping of rain on the windows. I started my lungs working again and slid into the drawing room. The darkness was like a black curtain hanging before my eyes, and I could not see even the outlines of the windows. I hesitated, afraid to move for fear of bumping into something, and conscious that I was perspiring freely from pure nervousness.

I lit a match after a while, and with the help of an entire book of them I made my way slowly down the length of the vast room and through its clutter of chairs, tables, footstools and fuzzy rugs. The succession of feeble little lights showed me that the tall, narrow windows were curtained with heavy drapes which were pulled right across them.

I reached the study door at last and went in with a sigh of relief. I could see the outlines of two windows here, and I pulled the drapes across them before lighting a match which guided me to a lamp standing on a desk in the middle of the room. I switched the lamp on and relaxed for a moment in its glow.

The room was sparsely furnished, and the desk seemed to be the only possible place for the letters. I closed the door through which I had just come and set to work.

It turned out to be more of a job than I had supposed. None of the drawers was locked, but they were crammed with papers of all sorts, and I had to go through them all. I didn't bother to read any of the papers or look at them closely; I wanted to get the letters in the shortest possible time and get out.

I was down on my knees, feverishly trying to finish the last drawer, when a voice spoke behind me.

"I doubt if you'll find them there," it said impersonally. "I looked myself."

I felt my heart stop dead and then begin to race madly as I stumbled to my feet.

Allan Barton stood just inside the door. He wore a dressing robe and was smoking a cigarette.

I swallowed twice, dropped a couple of papers that were still sticking clammily to my hands and asked in a queer, hollow voice, "How did you get here? Without my hearing you, I mean."

"Damned if I know," he said equably. "I made no particular effort to be quiet."

I couldn't think of any more small talk, so I just stood there, shivering and wondering what it would be like in jail.

He looked me over coolly and spoke again. "Handsome-looking garment you're wearing. Where did you get it? Fourteenth Street?"

I opened my mouth, but no sound came out, and he added, "Or was it Fifth Avenue, perhaps?"

Something that passed for an idea stirred in my brain, and I blinked several times and said loudly, "Where am I!"

Allan put the cigarette in his mouth and continued to regard me through the smoke.

I tried to look dazed and stammered out, "I'm very sorry, sir. I must have been sleepwalking. Been a habit ever since I was a nipper, sir."

He removed the cigarette and laughed nastily. "I suppose you deserve A for effort, but as an adventuress, your skill is away below par."

I sat down on a chair then and gave up. "Phone the police," I said wearily, "and let's get on with it."

His eyebrows shot up. "Police? But what about Selma? Won't she come forward and exonerate you?"

"Selma!" I said faintly and wondered how I could have forgotten her. Of course she'd have to get me out of this. But how had the man known?

"Who told you? That this was Selma's scheme, I mean?" I asked uncomfortably.

"Obvious," he said with a touch of impatience. "I've been wondering ever since you came how someone like you could possibly be a maid named Ellen McTavish. I heard someone go down the front stairs awhile ago, so I followed along to see who was so restless. I found the drawing-room doors open, saw a light under the door of my study and found you. And two and two always make four."

"I came down the back stairs," I said feebly.

"Then there's someone else down here," he replied, undisturbed.

I remembered suddenly and exclaimed, "Mr. George Barton. He's sitting in the dining room."

He showed no interest in the change of subject but asked pointedly, "Which drawer were you up to?"

"Well, I—I'd finished," I admitted and felt my face burning.

"Did you find those letters?"

"No."

He stirred and killed his cigarette in a bronze ashtray that lay on the desk. "Disappointing. I had hoped you'd turn them up."

"Do you mean you've lost them?"

"Oh no," he said easily, "they're around the house somewhere. I put them in a particularly safe place—only I can't remember where it was. I'm glad you've done this room; it saves me the trouble. Now tomorrow you can do my bedroom, because they might possibly be there."

"Tomorrow," I said, "I'm leaving—early." I stood up and tried to pass him, but he put an unexpectedly quick and purposeful hand on my shoulder.

"Just a minute."

"But—"

"I'll have to make sure that you haven't those letters on you."

Quickly and efficiently, before I knew what was happening, he felt me all over!

I don't think I've been so furious since I was born. I gave his face a resounding slap that seemed to ring through the silence like a gong, and then I had the sense to run.

I flew through the hall and around behind the stairs, where there was a closet. I shut myself in with rubbers, umbrellas, tennis rackets and a raincoat or two and waited, with my heart pounding uncomfortably.

I heard Allan come out of the drawing room and close the doors, and then he started up the stairs. When he was just about over my head I heard him laugh. It made me mad all over again, but I controlled myself to silence until his footsteps had died away on the second floor. I began to push the door open cautiously then but stopped abruptly halfway and had to retreat again. A man and a woman had come quietly into the corridor from the kitchen. It was too dark to identify them, but I heard them creep right up to the door of the closet, where they stopped. They executed something fancy in the way of a kiss then, and the man murmured, "Good night, sweetheart."

She said, "Darling! Darling!" in a slightly louder whisper, and the man muttered, "Shh."

They apparently separated then, and I heard his heavier step on the back stairs, while she tapped lightly up the front stairs. There was stealth and caution in both their movements.

I emerged from the closet, wiped the sweat from my brow and made for the back stairs. I noticed, as I passed the dining room, that George still sat at the table, but he seemed to be sleeping now, for his head had fallen forward onto his chest.

I crept up the back stairs and speculated with a good deal of interest on the identity of the lovers. But my musing was cut short. At the head of the stairs I nearly bumped into a tall, slim figure in white.

CHAPTER FIVE

JUST before I died of fright the thing spoke, and I recognized Franny's voice.

"What are you doing, Ellen, running around the house at this time of night?" she demanded in a hoarse whisper.

"Oh—why, just walking," I said idiotically. "Taking a walk, you know."

"Taking a walk! What do you mean? Explain yourself."

"I couldn't sleep," I said more coherently. "So I got up and took a walk around. The house is so—er—interesting."

"Did you meet anyone down there?" she asked abruptly and lowering the whisper a couple of tones.

"No. That is, Mr. Barton is in the dining room."

"Oh. Anybody else?"

I decided to keep out of the affairs of the two who had been love-making and said, "No."

"Which Mr. Barton is it in the dining room?"

"Mr. George Barton."

"What is he doing?"

"Just sitting at the table."

She brushed past me and seemed to be peering down the black well of the staircase. I left her to it and slipped off in the darkness to my own room.

I went straight to bed, but although I was desperately tired I could not sleep. I worried about having been found out so promptly, and I kept wondering uneasily what Allan was going to do about it. I decided at last to skip the place as early as I possibly could, and then I had to get out of bed and rummage in my purse for the timetable Selma had given me.

It seemed absolutely incredible, but the first train in the morning left at a quarter to five and the next at ten o'clock. I wasted some minutes in useless exasperation and then made up my mind to take the quarter to five. I felt that it would be the safer; I could creep out without seeing any of them again.

I went back to bed for a couple of hours of rest, and with my mind thus eased I presently fell asleep.

A persistent knocking on my door brought me back to consciousness, and I opened my eyes to full daylight. I jerked my head away from the pillow and saw, with horror, that the hands of the clock stood at a quarter to six.

I dropped my head back with a groan. I'd have to take the ten-o'clock train and I might run into all sorts of trouble before then. I half considered going to the station at once and abandoned it. They'd know where to find me and could easily come after me.

The knocking on my door continued monotonously, and I got out of bed and pulled it open. Jennie stood in the hall, and after a grim good morning she said, "You're late. Don't you know you're supposed to have the drawing room, study and sitting room all done before breakfast?"

"For heaven's sake, why?" I asked, astonished.

Her brow furrowed in a severe little frown, and she said sternly, "Those rooms will be in use during the morning, and you can't do them after breakfast."

It seemed absurd to me to rush my work through before breakfast when I had all day, but I didn't bother to argue. I told Jennie I'd dress at once, and she seemed satisfied. She went back to her room, and I could hear her chevying Mr. Keith. "Wake up, lazy bones," she said with grisly six-o'clock cheerfulness. "It's another day."

I glanced at the window and saw that it was still raining—lightly but steadily.

I got into my fancy maid's costume again and, after looking it over in the mirror, decided that it certainly was snappy. My shoes were nearly dry, and I put them on. They were the latest in spectator sports, but at that, I figured they looked better than the slippers. Bright red satin and rhinestones were, perhaps, a bit garish for the daytime.

Jennie came back and observed, "You'll get fired, for sure, if you don't get a move on."

"I'm all ready," I said hastily. "Come and show me what I have to do."

She nodded, and after pausing long enough to urge more speed on Mr. Keith she accompanied me to the kitchen. She showed me a large closet filled with brooms, dusters, pails and tools of that ilk and then told me where the various rooms were situated. Breakfast, she added, would be ready for us at seven-thirty, and the family breakfasted at eight-thirty.

"You don't need to vacuum today," she said, moving off toward the pantry. "Just the regular cleaning."

I rummaged in the closet for some time before I found the feather duster, and it turned out to be a rather motheaten object, with very few feathers left. I decided it would have to do, however, and went off to tackle the study first.

It didn't take a minute, and the drawing room was easy, too, except that I knocked a small china figure off the mantel and chipped a piece off its nose. But the thing was so hideous that it didn't bother me; in fact, I considered the chipped nose an improvement.

In the sitting room I found a few newspapers lying around, and some of the ashtrays were dirty. I supposed that it was my duty to tidy up a bit, so I stuffed the newspapers under the old-fashioned leather sofa and threw the ashes and butts out into the rain. I flipped the duster around—rather expertly, by that time—and returned to the kitchen, where I put the tool of my trade back into its closet. I sat down at the table then, lit a cigarette and wished that it was ten o'clock.

Jennie emerged from the pantry and gave me a surprised stare. "Heavens above, girl, what makes you think you have time to smoke?"

"Well, what else am I supposed to do?" I asked crossly. "I've finished those rooms, and I don't see why I should work like a dray horse before I have my breakfast."

"Do you mean to tell me you've finished those three rooms?"

"Certainly."

"Did you do them thoroughly?" she asked suspiciously.

"Of course. I went into every nook and cranny."

"I've never known it done in that short a time," she said, fixing me with her eye. "And we've had some shiftless females here in our time too."

I began to realize that there was more to this cleaning up than just the feather-duster business, and I heaped another mental curse on Selma's head.

"Well—but I work with lightning speed," I said defensively. "If Lord McNab were here he'd tell you the same thing. I was a byword in his household. He even showed me at the county fair."

Her eyes narrowed to mere slits, and she said coldly, "Lord who?"

"McNab. His first name was Sandy, but of course I never, got to call him by it. He—"

Mr. Keith came up from the cellar at this point and observed gravely, "Bit wet down there."

Jennie was diverted at once. She said, "Dear, dear! Mr. Allan will be upset, after him paying all that to have it fixed."

Mr. Keith shrugged and seated himself at the table, which was set for four. Jennie immediately placed a bowl of oatmeal before him and announced unnecessarily, "Here's your porridge, Mr. Keith."

I waited expectantly, but Jennie merely filled a bowl for herself, and the two of them started to eat.

"May I have some porridge too?" I asked politely. The stuff looked unappetizing, but I was starving.

"Help yourself, by all means," said Jennie hospitably.

I helped myself, and we began the rather solemn business of breakfasting. Eggs and bacon, tea, toast and marmalade followed the oatmeal, and I had got to the point of loosening my apron a trifle when a good-looking man, splendidly arrayed in a chauffeur's uniform, walked in.

He said breezily, "Morning, Keiths, A and B," and then he caught sight of me and stopped short. "Well, wadayaknow? Glamour girl—right here in the kitchen. Gladtaseeya, babe."

I nodded coldly and took out a cigarette.

Jennie said with sudden shrewishness, "Put that weed away. I'll have no woman smoking in my kitchen."

"Good thing the Bartons don't feel that way," I said carelessly as I lit up, "or they'd lose the fastest duster in the country."

Jennie seemed to lose her temper altogether. She snatched the cigarette out of my mouth and flung it into the sink. "Listen, you brazen little chit," she yelled, "you're not going to smoke here, and you can make up your mind to it."

Mr. Keith spoke sharply into the fracas. "Jennie!" he said. "It's after eight. Stop quarreling and attend to the breakfast."

She turned on him with her eyes blazing, and I thought she was going to hit him over the head, and then she glanced at the clock and started to bustle around the kitchen, getting breakfast. She shouted an order at me to go in and set the table.

I shrugged and departed for the dinning room, glad to get away from it all.

I pushed through the swinging door and then came to a gasping halt.

George Barton was still at the table, with his watch lying in front of him. His head hung forward on his chest, and a thick smear of coagulated blood covered the side of his face.

CHAPTER SIX

I FELT deathly sick for a moment, and then I turned and fled back to the kitchen.

Mr. Keith, who had been observing the rain, with his hands in his pockets, turned around and stared. Jennie raised a flushed, perspiring face from the stove and gazed at me in astonishment, and Oliver, the chauffeur, still breakfasting at the table, dropped his mouth open and sat with an entire egg yolk suspended midway between his mouth and his plate.

I struggled with my breath for a moment and then gasped, "Oh, quickly—somebody, come. Mr. Barton—in the dining room—"

Mr. Keith removed his hands from his pockets and made hastily for the dining room, and Jennie, dropping a spoon that made a sharp clatter in the silence, wiped her hands on her apron and ran after him. Oliver put the egg into his mouth, apparently to get rid of it, and followed them.

Mr. Keith returned after a few minutes and went straight to the kitchen telephone and summoned a doctor. He took time out to caution me to stay where I was and then hurried upstairs. I began to pace the floor restlessly, conscious all the time of the excited buzz of conversation coming from Jennie and Oliver in the dining room.

I looked out into the corridor after a while and saw Allan and Mr. Keith go into the dining room. I pulled my head back into the kitchen and continued to pace up and down.

When the doctor arrived at last, Jennie, Oliver and I all opened the door for him. He was an elderly man with gray hair and a red nose—but he never touched a drop, according to Jennie, who gave me a whispered outline of his life's history. It seemed he was a church member in good standing, with a wife who did her duty, a decently married daughter and a Ford car.

Jennie and I came to a halt at the dining-room door, but Oliver followed the doctor into the room.

Allan and Mr. Keith stood, one on each side of George, who remained in the same position.

Allan said, "I'm afraid it's no use, Doctor. He's dead."

Jennie, sensible of the proprieties, began to sob mournfully, while the doctor stooped over George Barton. He straightened again almost immediately and said, "Yes, yes. Been dead for some time. Er—shot, you know, Allan. Police matter, I'm afraid."

Jennie stopped sobbing at once, and her small eyes popped. Oliver gave a low whistle, but Allan and Mr. Keith remained poker-faced.

Allan nodded. "Yes, I know, but there's no weapon. We've looked."

The doctor said, "Hmm," and Mr. Keith murmured, "Shall I phone the police, sir?"

Allan and Dr. Wallace said, "Yes," and Mr. Keith faded away quickly.

Oliver was told to leave then, and Jennie and I saved our dignities by departing before we were told.

Mr. Keith presently joined us in the kitchen, and we discussed the thing with lively interest. Mr. Keith gave it as his opinion—in a low, grave voice—that it was undoubtedly murder, and Jennie gave a little scream.

Oliver gave his head a shake and muttered, "Jeez! I'm gettin' outa this joint. Who did it, Mr. Keith?"

"Nobody knows."

"Maybe it was suicide," I suggested hopefully.

Mr. Keith eased himself into a chair and explained it to us. "Suicide is out of the question. Mr. Allan and I looked for a gun, and there was nothing of the sort in the room. Further, I examined the wound carefully, and there were no powder marks. Therefore, he must have been shot from a distance of several paces at least."

Jennie stared at him in complete bewilderment and asked, "What are you talking about?" And Oliver chimed in, "Yeah. Where did you get the college education?"

"I have done a great deal of reading," said Mr. Keith loftily, "and I know what I'm talking about." He lighted his pipe, leaned back in his chair and gazed at the ceiling with half-closed eyes.

"You dames stop breathing for a while," Oliver jeered, "while the great guy dopes it out. He'll have it all ready, includin' the parsley, when the cops get here."

Allan walked into the kitchen at that point and said peremptorily, "Keith. Send breakfast up to Mrs. Barton and Miss Frances. Mr. Ross and I will have breakfast in the sitting room as soon as possible, please."

Mr. Keith dropped his pose at once and stood up, and Jennie began to bustle at the stove.

I was delegated to take the tray upstairs. I gathered that it was one of the duties, over and above feather-dusting, that Selma had neglected to mention.

I was given Hattie's tray first and told to hurry back for Franny's.

Hattie was the wife of the now-defunct George, and Selma had passed her over with the brief remark that she was much younger than George and was a mess.

I supposed that Allan had broken the news to her, and I hated going in with the tray, but it proved easier than I had expected. She was sitting up in bed, propped with pillows, and wore a frilly lace bed jacket. She appeared to be in her thirties somewhere, was too plump and had badly bleached hair. It was obvious she didn't care much about losing George, but I was convinced somehow that she was frightened.

She asked, "Who are you?" And I could see her eyes traveling over my natty uniform.

"I'm Ellen, the new maid," I explained, faintly impatient.

"Oh yes." She raised her eyes to my face and said, almost desperately, "Who killed my husband? Allan won't tell me—and I've got to know. I've got to."

"I don't believe anyone knows," I said, watching her curiously.

She said no more but dabbed at her eyes with a handkerchief which had a wide border of lace. I set the tray before her, and she tucked the handkerchief into the front of her nightgown and attacked the food in a businesslike fashion.

I returned to the kitchen and was given Franny's tray and stern instructions to hurry up about it, because there was plenty to do. All of which was a waste of Jennie's good breath, as it happened, because Franny kept me with her for all of an hour.

When I carried the tray into her room I found her standing in one of the darker corners, her eyes wide and glittering with fear. She looked like asylum material to me, and I came to a halt and eyed her warily.

She came out of her corner then and sharply ordered me to put the tray on the table. I lowered it with a clatter and streaked for the door, but she called after me shrilly and made me come back. She told me to sit down, and I perched uneasily on the window seat while she asked innumerable questions about George's demise. My own information was meager, but I repeated what I did know about six or seven times.

She did not touch her breakfast, and when I reminded her of it she seemed not to hear me. Several times she muttered, "It's dreadful!" And once, in a sort of despairing way, "What am I going to do?"

I left her at about twenty minutes to ten and hurried upstairs with an inspired determination to make a quick dash for the ten-o'clock train. I had a wishful hope that if I slipped out quietly I wouldn't be noticed.

I changed my clothes, flung my things into the overnight bag and sneaked quietly down.

I was halfway out the front door when Allan caught me. He simply hooked me by the arm and pulled me back into the hall again.

"Are you demented?" he asked in an exasperated voice. "Do you realize that my brother has been murdered? Even if you shot him yourself, your worst possible move would be to skip now. And take a look at the situation, if you're innocent. You came here under a false name—there is a murder immediately—and then you disappear. I have no interest in you or your affairs, but I suppose you're a friend of Selma's, and I'll do what I can to protect you. Now what's your real name?"

I had a strong impulse to give his face another ringing slap, but I think he saw it, for his hand tightened warningly on my arm.

I allowed the impulse to die and said furiously, "How dare you hint that I might have killed your brother."

He dropped his hand from my arm and said coldly, "Now look here. I have no idea who killed my brother, but I intend to do everything in my power to help the police find out. They'll question you, and if you tell them your name is Ellen McTavish they'll turn it up as a lie within a few hours. You'll be a damn sight more sensible if you give me your real name, so that I can explain to them that you're here to study a maid's part for the stage. In fact, it's possible that they may be able to keep your name out of it."

All the fight oozed out of me, and I heard myself saying feebly, "Would they believe it? That I'm studying a maid's part?"

He laughed. "No," he said. "I'll think up a better one. What's your name?"

"Callie Drake," I sighed.

"Callie? That's odd. What's it short for?"

I felt anger stirring in me again. My mother had picked my name—I had always thought it rather pretty—and it wasn't short for anything.

I tried to keep my temper and said sulkily, "Calisthenics."

He half closed his eyes and regarded me from under the lowered lids. "I don't care much for nicknames, so if you don't mind, I'll call you by your full name. You're a friend of Selma's?"

I swallowed and nodded dumbly.

"She sent you out here to pick up some letters that she claims are hers?"

I nodded again, miserably.

"I suppose she offered you something by way of payment?"

"It was part blackmail," I whispered, studying the carpet.

"Nevertheless, she offered you something? You must have wanted it pretty badly to do a thing like this. What was it?"

"Her roadster."

"You wanted Selma's roadster?"

"Yes."

He said, "Good God! Do you mean that vulgar white crate with the red leather seat?"

"I don't care what you think," I said desperately; "I want it. Maybe it is vulgar—"

"All right," he broke in, "I believe you—you want it. Now go on back upstairs and put yourself into that theatrical maid's costume again and go about your work. I'm going to phone Selma and check your story."

"Do you mean that I have to go on doing housework around here?" I asked in dismay.

"It's up to you. But I warn you that if you leave now, you'll very likely end up in jail."

He went off to his study then, and I slowly climbed the stairs to my room. I unpacked my bag and then went to the bathroom and drew a big, steaming hot bath. I was lying in it, comfortably soaking, when I noticed that the month of May had been ripped off the calendar, and it was showing June.

CHAPTER SEVEN

I FELT an uncomfortable prickling along my spine. I had forgotten about all the calendars with the fourteenth of May encircled—the day on which George Barton was to be murdered. I had a sudden panicky impulse to get out of the bath and get downstairs among people.

But I had company right away. There was a pounding on the door, and Jennie's voice asked fiercely, "Are you in there, Ellen McTavish?"

"I'm taking a bath," I said with dignity.

"You're what?" she shrieked.

"Hoot mon!" I yelled back and climbed out onto the linoleum-covered floor.

Jennie continued to stand outside, shrilling abuse, and when I had dried myself and resumed my robe she followed me to my room, telling me in great detail about all the work she had to do, and on top of that she had all mine to do as well—and Mr. George lying dead!

I interrupted her at that point. "If you have so much work to do," I said firmly, "you'd better run along and do it. As for my bath, I always took one at this time in the morning when I was with Lord McNab—and I'm not going to change my habits for a bunch of common Bartons."

It shut her up completely for a moment. Her mouth dropped open and she stared at me. When she spoke it was to say almost feebly, "You did?"

"Yes, I did."

She thought it over for a while, and then indignation covered her face like a blush. "They are not common," she said hotly.

"Who?"

"The Bartons. They're not common at all; they're very highly born."

"Not high enough," I said, slipping into my uniform. "The McNabs wouldn't look at them—except through a lorgnette."

I could see that Jennie was preparing to fight it to a finish, when Mr. Keith joined us. She started to tell him all about it, but he waved her to silence.

"This is no time for differences of opinion," he said. "We are all wanted downstairs—the police. Come on, Ellen."

I followed them downstairs with a sinking feeling at the pit of my stomach. I would have given anything to have been somewhere else—even Kansas.

In the kitchen Oliver stood by the window; a big, fat man lounged in one of the chairs, chewing gum and staring into space, and another man, slight, bald and wearing horn-rimmed spectacles, stood in front of the sink and stared at the calendar, which agreed with the one in the bathroom in proclaiming June.

He turned around as we came in and asked abruptly, "Who tore the May sheet off this calendar?"

There was a dead silence, and he asked impatiently, "Why was it torn off?"

I stepped forward, feeling pleasantly important, and said, "Maybe it was because somebody had circled yesterday's date in pencil."

Everybody stared at me, and the small man said, "There was a line drawn around yesterday's date?"

"Yes," I said, enjoying myself, "and there's a calendar in the servants' bathroom and one in the pantry. They both had yesterday's date circled, and May has been torn off the one in the bathroom."

The small man stepped into the pantry and reappeared again, nodding his head. "Torn off in there too." He looked at Mr. Keith. "What other calendars are there in the house?"

Mr. Keith said, after thought, that there was one each in the living room, the study and Mr. Allan's bedroom. "That's all, I believe, Mr. Hatton."

Mr. Hatton grunted and cast a glance on the fat individual. "Go and see what those calendars look like now, Bill."

Bill said, "O.K., boss," and heaved himself off the chair.

Mr. Hatton began to question us then about what time we had all gone to bed the night before.

I answered briefly and decided to leave out my nocturnal visit to the study. Oliver said he had come in at about eleven-thirty, and Jennie and Mr. Keith thought they had returned at about ten-thirty. Jennie added that they had been delayed in the kitchen because the housemaid had gone upstairs and left everything lying.

Mr. Hatton swung his horn rims around on me and asked me why I had gone off and left everything lying.

I explained that I had had a headache but had returned to the kitchen later, only to find everything done.

"Nice timing," said Mr. Hatton.

Mr. Keith cleared his throat tentatively. "Er—Mr. Hatton—"

Unexpectedly Mr. Hatton blew up. His face became suffused with dark red, and his voice rose to a high treble. "Will you kindly stop calling me *mister?*" he spluttered. "It's *detective—Detective* Hatton."

Mr. Keith maintained his dignity. He glanced at his nails, smoothed his hair and quietly studied the ceiling.

Detective Hatton presently recovered himself and asked, "What were you going to say, Keith?"

But Mr. Keith, though clothed in dignity, was offended, nevertheless.

"I merely wished to observe that it is still raining," he said coldly.

An apparent incipient apoplexy in Detective Hatton was checked by Bill's return.

"All them calendars," said Bill cheerfully, "have May torn off."

Detective Hatton decided to leave us at this point, but he warned us that we were to be questioned separately and at length after lunch.

Jennie heaved a great sigh after he had gone and declared that she never had liked policemen. "What would you like for your lunch, Mr. Keith?"

"A little of the roast beef," said Mr. Keith absently and left the kitchen.

"Tell me something," I said to Jennie as soon as the door had closed behind him. "Why do you call him Mr. Keith? He's your husband, isn't he?"

"Are you calling my respectability into question, miss?" she demanded belligerently. "He's my husband, all right, and don't you dare—"

"All right," I said impatiently. "But why do you have to call him mister?"

"I don't *have* to," she snapped. "It's just out of respect—that's all. Here—you go and lay the table."

I met Bill in the dining room, and he told me that he could go for me if I gave him the wink.

I said I was sorry but I already had a steady.

Bill said, "Oh, don't be old fashioned. Even if you was married, it ain't gonna hurt anybody if you go out with another guy, is it?"

"Oh," I said. "You want to take me out."

"Sure. How about the movies tonight?"

Apparently he heard the approach of Detective Hatton at that moment—although certainly I didn't—and in a flash he was down on his hands and knees, studying the carpet under the table. The detective walked in and looked first at me and then at what he could see of Bill. "What are you doing under there?" he asked irritably.

"Thought I saw something, chief," Bill said, crawling out again.

"Well, don't bother thinking; you can leave that to me."

He sent Bill out of the room then and proceeded to tell me that he knew all about me. Mr. Allan Barton had told him everything, and he was going to try to keep my real name out of the proceedings if it was at all possible. By way of return he wanted the fullest cooperation from me.

I promised it with all my heart and soul and thanked him warmly into the bargain.

During lunch I was sent up to the bedrooms, and I went straight to Allan's room, with a vague idea of finding those letters and earning Selma's roadster. But honor got the better of me. I reflected that Allan had pulled me out of a nasty situation, and the least I could do was to leave his letters alone. I decided simply to clean the room in the manner of a good housemaid.

It was not an easy job. There were a lot of things lying around, which I finally disposed of by throwing them into the closet. Next I attempted to make the bed and discovered that it was simply impossible. I knew how a bed should lock when properly made, but I could not get it into that condition. I pulled the top cover up tightly, at last, and decided to insist fiercely that that was the way it was done at Lord McNab's, when I was tackled about it.

The other rooms went faster. Franny came in while I was doing hers and, seating herself in a rocker, proceeded to chew nervously at her nails. "I don't know what to do," she said after a while in a sort of low moan. "I simply don't know what to do."

I asked her if I could help her in any way—I felt sorry for her somehow—but she only shook her head and continued to rock monotonously.

Fortunately she didn't notice the way I had made her bed at all, and just as I was preparing to leave she said suddenly, "If only Allan would let me have a dog—I'd like a big dog—to protect me."

I paused with my hand on the door and said in some surprise, "But surely he'd let you get a dog if you want one."

"No, no—you don't understand," she said tiredly. "George had a horror of animals, and Allan always backed him up when it was a question of pets in the house. I know he won't allow me to have a dog."

I left her with an uneasy feeling that she was cracking under the strain, and I felt that I'd better go and tell Allan about her.

I found him in his study, and he appeared to be in a thoroughly irritable humor. "What is it now?" he snapped. "I've had plenty of trouble over you, and I expect plenty more."

I was hurt and decided at once to go on with my search for the letters. "I think Miss Barton wants some attention," I said in an offended voice. "She seems to be wandering a bit."

He said, "Thank you," briefly, and I turned and went out.

Jennie caught up with me in the back corridor and wanted to know just how much longer she was expected to try and keep my lunch hot for me. Further, she branded as a deliberate lie my earlier assertion that I had cleaned the lower rooms before breakfast. They were in a disgraceful state, and I would have to do them properly during the afternoon.

I ignored her and went on to the kitchen to pick up my lunch.

Mr. Keith and Oliver were lounging comfortably with their pipes, and they both nodded courteously to me. Oliver removed his pipe long enough to invite me to the movies that evening.

I tossed my head and said carelessly, "I have a date for the movies tonight."

"Whosa guy?" Oliver asked, surprised.

"Bill."

"Bill who?"

"Just Bill," I said airily. "He works for Mr. Detective Hatton."

"He works fast too," Oliver muttered.

Hattie walked into the kitchen just then, and I was amazed to think that she could have been married to a man like George. She looked thoroughly cheap. She wore a tweed skirt and checked jacket which increased the width of her heavy hips, and her face appeared to have two or three coats of paint on it.

She said, "Oliver, bring the car around. I want you to take me out for a while. I have some errands."

"Yes, madam," Oliver said sulkily. Jennie and Mr. Keith exchanged a long, significant look.

Hattie started for the door but I think she must have felt the Keiths' silent disapproval, for she stopped and turned on Jennie. "Oh, I know what you're thinking," she said, her voice high and not quite steady, "but I don't believe in going into mourning. I can feel just as bad in anything else."

She went out and closed the door with a swish, and Oliver got up slowly and felt in his pocket for a toothpick. He lounged out the back door, idly picking his teeth.

I lit a cigarette, and as Jennie's mouth opened I jumped in ahead of her. "Shut up!" I said loudly, "and attend to your own affairs. I'm going to smoke in here whenever I please."

For a moment a real battle hung in the balance, and then she subsided into sulky muttering. She was still grumbling when I left the kitchen five minutes later.

I made for my bedroom, determined to have a nice long nap. I was a little startled at my identification of Hattie and Oliver as the two who had been making love in the back corridor the night before, but there was no doubt about it. I was sure of their voices. I decided that Oliver was some kind of a skunk.

I looked my room over with a newly professional eye and saw that it was thick with dust. I shrugged and reflected that it could wait until somebody had to take a shovel to it. I moved over to the bureau and picked up my comb and stood, holding it halfway to my hair.

There was, on the dusty surface of that bureau, the distinct mark of an animal's paw.

CHAPTER EIGHT

THERE WAS a plain white scarf on the bureau, but it was narrow and showed a strip of the varnished wood on each side. The mark was in the front strip, close to the edge, and I was able to study it carefully. It was certainly the print of an animal's paw, but it was neither a squirrel nor a rat; it was much too large. And there was only one.

I found myself shivering with cold and fear. The house seemed a place of horror, and I was trapped there by my own stupidity in having come at all.

I took refuge in another hot bath, and it warmed me and seemed to give me courage to face my obligations to Allan and Detective Hatton.

On my way out of the bathroom I ran into Jennie, who exhibited the usual mixture of astonishment and anger.

"Have you just had another bath?" she demanded, with the surprised contempt of one who bathes regularly every Saturday night.

I nodded coldly.

"What do you think you are?" she asked, following me so closely that she almost stepped on my heels. "A movie star, or something? If you think I'm going to put up with—"

I interrupted thoughtfully, "Say, Jennie "

"Mrs. Keith to you," she snapped.

"All right—Mrs. Keith. Are there any dogs or cats in this house?"

"There are no dogs," said Jennie, "and only one cat—and that's you."

"No other kind of cats, besides me?"

Indignation gave way to curiosity, and she asked, "What are you trying to get at? Mr. Keith and I would give notice at once if they tried bringing any pets here."

She went off then before I could show her the mark on my bureau and flung over her shoulder that she was going to report me at once.

I dressed leisurely and went downstairs, where I was promptly gathered in by Detective Hatton. He questioned me thoroughly and fortunately prefaced the proceedings by telling me why I was there. It seemed I was a member of a serious-minded group of women who were making a study of the servant situation. Several of us were working as servants in the homes of friends, in order to get friendly with the other servants and find out their grievances and just what it was they did when they had to get even with their employers about something.

Detective Hatton took me slowly and carefully over the night before, and I answered readily enough. But I closed my account with the statement that I had gone to bed after coming upstairs with the Keiths, so that my seeing George in the dining room, Allan in the study and Hattie and Oliver in the corridor was all left out. I hoped that Allan had said nothing about having seen me and figured that he might keep silent to hide his own trip downstairs.

Apparently he had done just that, because Detective Hatton seemed quite satisfied with my story and presently dismissed me.

I had been questioned in the sitting room, and when I walked out into the hall Jennie was waiting for me. She had a sort of cat-and-saucer-of-cream expression.

"Mr. Allan wants you," she said, almost gleefully. "In the study—immediately."

"Tattletale!" I said, making a face at her. "I'm not afraid of him."

I went to the study, where I found Allan writing at his desk. I sat down and said, "Jennie says you want to see me."

He glanced at me and said briefly, "Stand up."

I stood up. "What for?" I asked in some surprise.

"It is customary for a servant to remain standing when she is talking to her employer."

I said, "For heaven's sake, don't be so petty."

"And kindly remember to append a 'sir,' when you address me."

"Listen, Mr. Barton," I said desperately, "all fooling aside—can't I possibly get away from here?"

"Also," he continued imperturbably, "I prefer that the servants call me 'Mr. Allan.' It's more friendly."

"You're about as friendly as a cobra," I said bitterly.

He threw down his pen and stood up. "Now listen to me. You can't leave here yet. I asked Detective Hatton about it, and he was emphatic that you remain for a while, at least. While you're here you'll get along with Jennie with a minimum of friction and do willingly whatever she asks. You will take no more than one bath a day—and that not during working hours. And you will not smoke in the kitchen. If I have any more trouble with you I'll wash my hands of the thing and simply tell Detective Hatton that you came here to steal some letters from me."

I was completely floored. I stared at him for a moment of silence and then struggled feebly into speech.

"Yes, sir, Mr. Allan, sir. I understand. Mr. Allan, could I get you some afternoon tea, sir?"

"Get out," he said shortly.

I got out, and all the way to the kitchen I reflected on what a cold, hard place the world was, and if I ever got back under my parents' wings I'd stay there forever.

Jennie was waiting for me in the kitchen, and her little eyes had a triumphant gleam.

I smiled at her from ear to ear. "Darling!" I said. "You should have told me!"

She backed away a step and asked warily, "Told you what?"

"Why, that you didn't like it when I took those baths and smoked in the kitchen. My *dear,* I wouldn't have *dreamed—*"

"What are you talking about?" she yelled, her face flushing angrily. "Are you daft?"

Mr. Keith came in just then and, waving our foolish woman's talk to silence, stated gravely, "Mr. Allan's gun is missing."

"How do you know?" Jennie whispered, the color fading from her face and leaving it unusually pale.

"I have just looked."

"Where did you look?" I asked.

"Where he always keeps it. The drawer of that table in the sitting room."

"How many people knew that it was there?" I asked, feeling like Detective Hatton.

"Everyone in the house, I believe," Mr. Keith said thoughtfully. "You knew, Jennie?"

She nodded. "It's been there for years, I guess. I knew about it when he bought that silencer thing. I remember he took it out in the back yard and shot at trees to see if the silencer worked."

"And did it work?"

They both nodded their heads. Jennie said, "Sure—pretty well, anyway. But he put it away in the drawer after that, and I don't think anyone has touched it since."

"Was it loaded while it was in the drawer?" I asked curiously.

"I don't know," Mr. Keith said, "but there has always been a box of bullets in the same drawer."

"Pretty careless, if you ask me," I said, shaking my head. Mr. Keith shrugged, and Jennie muttered, "It was that."

I was put to work cleaning silver then, and I managed to stretch it out until it was time to set the table for dinner.

Mr. Keith supervised my table setting, and he was so fussy about every smallest detail that I thought it would have been better all around if he had done it himself. I didn't suggest it to him though; I thought I'd better do what I was told and keep out of trouble.

When the meal was ready I found that I was expected to help Mr. Keith with the serving.

"But, Jennie," I protested helplessly, "I can't do it. I don't know how. I'm sure to make some frightful blunder."

"Do you mean to tell me," she said harshly, "that you never helped the butler at Lord McNab's?"

I drew myself up. "Of course not. There were half a dozen footmen, and no woman was tolerated in the dining room—except as a guest, of course."

Jennie said, "Well, I never!" But she made me go through with it just the same. She promised that Mr. Keith would give me the wink if I did anything wrong.

They all came down to dinner, including the blond and handsome Mr. Ross Barton, identified by Jennie as Mr. Allan's younger brother. I looked them over and came to the conclusion that of all the people in the room, Mr. Keith and I were the best dressed, and I was strongly inclined to think that we were the most aristocratic looking as well.

Allan and Ross wore undistinguished-looking dark business suits, and the two women were draped in tired-looking black silk daytime dresses.

Hattie had been crying, and her face was swollen and blotchy under the paint. The men were silent and almost morose, and Franny plucked constantly at the tablecloth. Hattie waded through a huge meal, but the others ate practically nothing.

I was nervous but I made only one break. I tried to save time by picking up Hattie's and Franny's plates at the same time, one in each hand. Something made me glance at Mr. Keith, and although not one feature of his face shifted position in the slightest degree, he yet managed to give me a look of such deadly menace that I nearly dropped the plates onto their two heads.

The family broke into low-voiced talk when Mr. Keith and I were out of the room and always stopped abruptly when we returned.

These tactics did not bother Mr. Keith in the slightest, however. As soon as the swinging door had settled into place he glued his ear to the crack and listened carefully, without losing any portion of his dignity, either. I tried to edge up beside him and listen, too, but he sternly motioned me away.

Jennie frowned at me. "The very idea! Haven't you any manners, girl?"

Oliver came in later, looking sulkier than ever, and while we were having our own dinner Mr. Keith told us something of what he had heard.

"They're worried about the gun. They found out it was missing, and Mr. Allan told the detective. Seems they've all been searching for it."

"Did they find it?" Jennie asked with her mouth full.

"No. There's to be an inquest tomorrow at ten, and we have to go."

Jennie moaned, "Good godfathers! I can't go; I've nothing to wear."

Oliver gave voice to a jeering laugh. "You women! Closets full of clothes, and nothing to wear." He left us as soon as he had finished his meal, but took time to observe, from the door, "Betcha that Bill stands you up."

"You got a date with that Bill?" Jennie asked.

"Yes, but as it happens, he'll have to stand up himself. I'm dead tired and I'm going to bed."

"Tired!" Jennie shrilled. "Mercy on us, what have you to be tired about? You haven't lifted your hand to a thing all day."

It seemed to me that I had been laboring from dawn until dark, but I didn't argue about it. As soon as everything had been cleared away I went straight up to my room with the firm intention of taking time only to lock my door and drop my clothes onto the floor before I dived for the bed.

I was balked right at the start. When I opened my door and switched on the light it was to find Franny huddled in the creaking old rocking chair, slowly swinging herself back and forth.

CHAPTER NINE

I REMAINED by the door and eyed Franny uneasily. I felt sure now that she was a bit unbalanced.

She stopped rocking and said to me with a certain amount of dignity, "I'm sorry to bother you, but I'm very nervous and I want to stay with you tonight."

It was the last thing that I wanted. I didn't feel at all sure that she wouldn't do me some damage while I slept. I glanced at the single bed and said uncomfortably, "But, Miss Barton, I'm afraid there isn't room, and you've only a single bed downstairs too."

She said, "Hush! Lower your voice. I don't want anyone to know I'm here."

"Why don't you sleep in with Miss Hattie?" I suggested in a loud whisper.

"Oh, no. No. I couldn't sleep in poor George's bed. That would be dreadful."

"But what can we do then?" I said helplessly. "We can't both sleep in a single bed."

She set the chair into motion again and said, "Don't fret yourself, child; I shall stay in this chair. It's all I want. I know I'll be safe here."

"Safe!" I repeated. "What do you mean, Miss Franny? Are you in danger?"

"Yes, I'm in danger," she said in a muffled voice and without looking at me. "You must let me stay here."

"But you can't sit up all night."

"I can and will," she snapped and began to rock herself furiously.

I gave up the argument, said, "All right" mildly and began to undress, wondering what on earth I was to do about her.

I got into my robe and slippers and decided, in the end, to take the whole thing to Allan. I told Franny I was going to the bathroom, and I went on down to the second floor and knocked on Allan's door.

Ross opened it, and after one comprehensive look at me and my costume he gave a long whistle and flung the door wide. "I am sorry, old man," he said to Allan, who had appeared behind him. "I should have left when you tried to hint me out a little while ago."

I ignored him coldly, hating him, and Allan said shortly, "Don't be a damn fool." He turned to me and asked crossly, "What do you want now? Permission to search the room so that you can still have a chance at that roadster?"

I swallowed down something else and said, "Oh no, sir. I wouldn't make so bold. It's about Miss Franny, sir."

I told them all about it, and both their expressions changed. They followed me upstairs in silence.

Franny was thoroughly put out when she saw them and inclined to cling desperately to her rocker, in spite of them. "I wish you'd just let me stay here. I'm not doing any harm. I want to stay here, because I know I'll be safe."

"What makes you think you're not safe?" Allan interrupted sharply.

"George wasn't safe," Franny snapped back.

Ross broke in pacifically, "Listen, Franny, you can sleep in peace. There's only a bathroom between our rooms, and we'll leave the connecting doors open so that you've only to shout if you want me."

She went along with them then, but I could see that she was still reluctant. As they reached the door Ross looked over his shoulder and deliberately winked at me. I kept my expression flat and unresponsive.

As soon as they had gone I fell into bed and then had to crawl out again, because I had forgotten about locking the door.

I discovered, rather to my horror, that there was no lock of any sort on the door and that it would not even close properly. It just met the jamb and would not be forced further. I pushed at it helplessly for a while and then left it in complete exasperation and went back to bed. I told myself earnestly that nobody would bother with me, anyway. I didn't even know them.

I was tired and I slept—a sort of close-to-the-surface sleep that was troubled with unpleasant dreams. I drifted back to consciousness with the sound of rain in my ears and the black night like a curtain in front of my eyes. I lay quite still and picked out the vague shape of the bureau and heard the ticking of the alarm clock. And then I realized that there was another sound in the room, and I was suddenly wide awake and sweating clammily. I could hear, quite plainly, the rhythmic creak of the old rocker.

I scrambled wildly out of bed and turned on the light. Franny was there, hunched into the rocker, swaying back and forth and looking at me with eyes like bits of dull glass.

"Oh, Miss Franny!" I gasped. "You gave me an awful scare."

"I'm sorry," she said unemotionally. "You should have let me stay here in the first place. I'm not safe anywhere else. But I'm all right in here with you."

"You could lock yourself in downstairs," I said desperately. "This door has no lock, and it doesn't even close properly."

"It doesn't matter—locks don't matter. I'm safe only while I'm with you. I won't be touched while I'm with you. But I wish you hadn't told anyone."

I began to pace the room restlessly, wondering what I ought to do, and came to the conclusion at last that I'd better call Allan again.

I told Franny that I was going to the bathroom, but this time she got up immediately, and said she'd go with me. We fooled around the bathroom for a while and then we returned to my room.

I got back into bed, because there did not seem to be anything else to do. Franny began to rock herself again, and after a while I fell asleep.

When I woke again the room was gray, and Franny was still rocking, but she looked pretty exhausted. I got up, wondering if I'd ever have enough sleep again, and began to dress. Jennie presently banged on the door and called cheerfully, "Time to get up."

Franny gave me a warning look and put her finger to her lips. I nodded, and when I had finished dressing I went on downstairs, leaving her there, still swaying slowly.

Jennie took no chances with my before-breakfast work this time. She went along with me, told me exactly what to do and how to do it, and left me with an armful of houseworker's tools. Nor was there a feather duster in the lot.

I toiled my way slowly through the drawing room, and I was still knee-deep in the study when Jennie came after me to announce breakfast. "You certainly are awful slow," she said and clicked her tongue. "I had to lay the table myself."

"Why didn't you get Mr. Keith to do it?" I asked, mopping at my hot face.

"Mr. Keith never does any such menial work as that," she said sharply. She proceeded to pass a couple of catty remarks about the way Lord McNab's household was run, which made me quite indignant. But discretion kept me silent.

After breakfast we had to get ready to go to the inquest. My uniform was pretty dirty by that time, so I changed into my dress and Selma's old raincoat. I had no hat, of course, and since it was still raining, I gave thanks for the fact that my hair curled naturally.

Jennie, Mr. Keith, Oliver and I all went in one car, and the family in another. The family left first, and we did not see them again until we got to the small county courthouse.

I noticed at once that Hattie had plunged into mourning. It appeared to be a brand-new outfit, and her head and shoulders were draped dramatically in yards of black veiling.

Oliver, following my eyes with his own, leaned over and whispered into my ear, "She bought all that junk yesterday."

Somebody had evidently pried Franny loose from my rocking chair, for she drooped beside Hattie, looking scared and miserable. She wore a black dress and a black hat that may have looked well enough when she bought them in nineteen ten.

The inquest was boring and seemed interminable. The same questions were asked over and over again, and had it not been for Hattie and Jennie, the audience—who had come in their Sunday clothes and prepared for a good time—would have been doomed to disappointment.

Jennie was called directly after I had stepped down. After a few preliminaries she was asked if she slept well.

On her face surprise gave way to deep concentration. "I don't rightly know," she said after a while. "I ain't had a chance to compare—"

She was sharply interrupted. "Would you know about it if your husband left the room at night?"

Jennie's face cleared, and she said, "Oh yes, of course."

"Why 'of course'?"

"Well, we have our toes tied together."

The spectators found this vastly entertaining, and I glanced at Mr. Keith to see how his dignity received the blow. His hands were folded, and he was gazing at the ceiling with a grave and thoughtful expression, as though he were unconscious of the rabble around him.

Jennie was explaining about the toes. "Mr. Keith sometimes walks in his sleep, and if he gets out of bed, of course it wakes me, and then I can wake him."

"But Keith could untie the string and go out without disturbing you?"

"I don't know," Jennie said doubtfully. "He never has done that."

She was asked then if she had heard Oliver come in, and she said no.

Hattie was called last, and she made quite a stir and a rustle with her weeds.

After the usual questions she was asked at what time her husband usually retired.

"He used to go to bed about ten," Hattie said readily, "but for the last month he has been sitting in the dining room until two o'clock every night."

"Why?"

"I don't know. I asked him about it, but all he would say was that it was the Lord's mission."

"Did he appear to be frightened in any way?"

"No," said Hattie, fingering her veil, "but he did happen to let drop that Sunday would be the last night he'd have to sit up."

"Do you know whether it was he who drew the circles on the calendars?"

"I don't know."

The questions were uninteresting for a while, and then she was asked, "Do you know of *anyone* who could explain why your husband sat up in the dining room night after night?"

"Oh yes," Hattie said easily. "He told me. Franny knew all about it."

CHAPTER TEN

FRANNY was recalled immediately, but they got exactly nowhere with her. She declared that she did not know what they were talking about, that she knew nothing about anything, and then she fainted.

We all went home after that. Franny was put to bed, and I was put to work. I had never before realized how lucky I was that my parents had money, and while I was lying on the floor, dusting behind a radiator, I made a solemn vow to marry a rich man as soon as possible. In the meantime I hoped desperately that the present nightmare would be over in a few days.

Jennie announced lunch after a while, and I was allowed barely time to gulp it down, when I was put back to work again.

It was close to four o'clock when Jennie sought me out, quivering with indignation. "You never finished the study," she said, as though it were grand larceny.

"Well," I said mildly, "as you know, breakfast interfered with that."

"Hear the girl! Breakfast, indeed. Why—"

I said wearily, "Let us keep our heads in this emergency. I'll finish the study now, instead of taking my bath."

"You'll not be taking any baths at this time of day," she yapped indignantly. "You march along and finish up that study."

I marched while she took herself back to the kitchen, muttering darkly all the way.

A small, cheerful wood fire burned in the study, and two easy chairs were drawn up on each side of it. No one was in the room, or in the drawing room behind me, and it didn't take me half a second to decide what to do. I relaxed into one of the chairs, lit a cigarette and stretched my feet to the blaze of the fire. The rain made a comfortable, low patter against the windows, and peace descended on me. The combination was fatal, and I promptly went off to sleep.

Some sort of subdued sound brought me back to consciousness, and I stirred and opened my eyes. Allan was sitting in the other easy chair. He was not looking at me but was staring into the fire with a rather somber expression. I wondered sleepily if he hadn't noticed me, and after that ridiculous thought I woke up completely.

He had a highball in his hand, and I saw that another stood on a low table between us. He glanced up at me as I moved and said, "Oh, you're awake."

I said, "Er—yes. I sat down to get a better view of the ceiling—looking for cobwebs, and—"

"And went to sleep and burned a hole in the carpet with your cigarette. But you must not be upset. The carpet can be mended, and I realize that my employees must sleep when they are sleepy."

I stood up. "I'm very sorry, sir. I'll darn the carpet myself."

"Sit down," he said briefly. "I want to talk to you."

I sat down, glad of any chance to rest in that house, where chances for rest were all too few.

He said, "You may smoke, and you may polish off the drink beside you if you care to."

"Oh, *thank* you, sir," I said gratefully. "It's right kind and thoughtful. I do miss me little nip of an afternoon."

He looked at me from under slightly lowered lids and said casually, "Be sure you don't use any sarcasm on me. I might get mad."

I picked up the highball, lit a cigarette and settled back with a sigh of pure pleasure. We smoked and drank in silence for quite a long time. Allan continued to stare at the fire, and I thought about my comfortable room at the hotel. He got up rather absentmindedly when I had finished the first cigarette and handed me another, and then he refilled both our glasses.

I was beginning to get a little uneasy by that time, and I watched him apprehensively as he resumed his chair. He set his glass down, and after a short silence he spoke. "What did you do, where did you go and whom did you see after you left me on Sunday night?"

"Well, I—you know, I didn't mention any of that to the police."

"I know."

"Do you think I should have?" I asked anxiously.

"No, I don't believe so," he said slowly. "I said nothing about it myself. But I'm beginning to think now that they should be told, and I want to know exactly what you saw or did. Try and remember everything, will you?"

I sat back, frowning in an effort at concentration, and had opened my mouth to begin, when Jennie burst into the room. She stopped dead at sight of us, and her little eyes bulged.

Allan spoke to her in a voice of cold fury. "Jennie, you are not to come into this room at any time without knocking. And in the future you will manage the distribution of work in the house more efficiently. I found this girl unconscious, and she is only now coming out of it. Now get out."

Jennie murmured, "I am sorry, sir; I'm sure I never meant anything," and backed out hastily.

Allan got up and refilled his glass. "I was fond of old George," he said, "even if he was a drip."

I swallowed a grin and realized that he must have been drinking for some time, since he would never so far have loosened his tongue to me otherwise.

He resumed his seat and said abruptly, "Go on—let's have it."

I told him the whole thing, including the love interest as provided by Hattie and Oliver.

He seemed genuinely disturbed by that and asked, "Are you sure it was Hattie and Oliver?"

"Absolutely sure. I did not see them again until the next day, but as soon as I heard them speak I was quite certain."

He frowned and made a restless movement. "But why would they stage their damned love scene in the hall there, when George was supposedly awake and sitting within a few yards of them?"

"Oliver was trying to shut Mrs. Barton up," I explained. "She was the one who didn't seem to care."

"You haven't repeated this to anyone else?"

"Not a soul," I assured him.

He looked at me oddly and said, "That was nice of you. I'll have to grant you your morning bath, or something."

"I'd rather have a straight eight-hour day."

"No servants' union to enforce it," he said and got himself another drink. He took a look at my empty glass then and filled it too. "That's all for you," he said, setting it down with a slight bang. "All you're going to get. Can't have you getting drunk. As for me, I'm not supposed to drop tears because I'm a man. So I'm going to get soused."

I was feeling a bit high myself, and something told me I ought to go, but of course I didn't.

"When is your divorce coming off?" I asked chattily.

"Now. Tomorrow. I won't appear, and Selma should be able to push it through all right."

"Tomorrow!" I gasped and looked despairingly at a mental picture of my roadster disappearing around a corner.

"Somewhat unexpected," he said, watching me, "but just as well. Selma will probably want to marry again, and there's no sense in her having to wait around."

"What about you? Do you want to marry again?" I asked and knew that I must be a bit tight.

"Oh yes," he said easily. "But there's no one in sight at the moment. You wouldn't do."

"My dear fellow," I said carefully, so that my tongue wouldn't trip, "I wouldn't want you at all."

"Is that so?" he asked politely.

"Yes." I sipped at my drink and thought uneasily of Mr. Keith being obliged to lay the table himself.

"I wouldn't mind taking you to the movies though," Allan said carelessly.

I finished my highball, decided that I felt fine and stood up. "Very sorry, I'm sure," I said, smoothing down my dress, "but I have dates with Oliver and Mother Hatton's helper, Bill, and I wouldn't be able to sandwich you in."

"No?"

"No."

He stood up and followed me to the door. "You will not," he said quietly, "go to the movies—or anywhere else—with either Oliver or Bill, the mother's helper."

"No?"

"No," he said. "I'll make it my business to see that they're both too busy."

I left him standing at the door of the study and wended my way, with surprising difficulty, through the overfurnished drawing room. I was surprised and annoyed to discover that I could not keep a straight course, and after I had made the kitchen I sank into a chair.

Jennie turned around from the stove and said, "Here! What's all this about you fainting?"

"And didn't you cop it?" I said and found myself laughing too loudly. I pulled myself together and added with dignity, "I came over a little weak and faint. But I'm here in time to set the table, you see."

"I see," she said grimly. "Go on—you'd better get busy. And let me tell you something. If you have any idea of setting your cap at Mr. Allan, you've got another think coming."

"You never know, lovey," I said, heading for the dining room. "I may be your mistress yet."

I went through the serving pantry in a hurry and pushed through the swinging door into the dining room. Mr. Keith was not there, and it was left to me to figure out alone just what tools and appurtenances were necessary for the feeding of four people. I had a skittish desire to find four bags, fill them with bread and put one at each place around the table and leave it at that. The idea kept me laughing quietly for five minutes, but I knew I was in no condition to follow anything but sober routine, so I pulled out tablecloth and silver and set to work.

I returned to the kitchen, accompanied by a conviction that I had forgotten several things. Mr. Keith was there, dressed for service in the dining room, smoking his pipe and holding forth to Jennie.

"—and so far as I can make out, they don't know who killed him. But here's something peculiar: it seems he was killed around twelve o'clock."

"Heavens alive!" Jennie exclaimed. "We didn't go up to bed much before that."

"We went up at eleven-twenty," Mr. Keith said distinctly. "We were in bed by eleven-thirty, and we were asleep before twelve o'clock."

"And I was downstairs," I thought to myself, "and so was Allan and so were Hattie and Oliver, and in amongst all that crowd someone slipped into the dining room and shot George." I shivered and had a moment of panic when I wished desperately that I was safely back with my parents.

Dinner was served in almost total silence. They were all there: Hattie and Franny, Ross and Allan, but they had nothing to say to each other even when Mr. Keith and I were out of the room.

At the conclusion of the meal Ross stood up and announced that he could not stand the house any longer and was going to drive to the nearest large town and find something to do. Hattie immediately showed signs of animation and said she'd go, too, but Ross shook his head and explained that he wasn't going anywhere where she could properly accompany him. Hattie's eyes were hard, and she turned to me and told me to send Oliver to her. I delivered this message, and Oliver took time to scowl blackly before he went in to her.

Hattie told him to bring the car around, as she was going to the movies. She carefully iced the order before giving it, and I decided that she and Oliver must have had a quarrel.

Franny spoke up at this point and gave it as her opinion that Hattie ought to stay at home and attend to her mourning. To be seen at the movies under the circumstances, Franny observed, was in very low taste. Hattie did not take the trouble even to answer.

Allan ignored them all completely, and I knew he was quite drunk.

Jennie and I cleared up, as usual, and I decided that if you were going to be a servant it was much better to be a male servant.

I put this view before Jennie, but she merely observed that if God had made you a female in the first place, you couldn't possibly hope to be a male servant.

I went straight upstairs after we had finished, and as I approached my room I heard the swish and creak of the rocking chair. I groaned inwardly and resigned myself to being stuck with Franny again.

But it was not Franny in my rocking chair; it was no one at all. And the empty chair, still swaying a little, eased to a stop as I stood there watching it.

CHAPTER ELEVEN

I stood just inside the room, staring at the rocker and feeling a scream collecting at the back of my throat. I swallowed it at last, for no better reason than that Jennie and Mr. Keith would undoubtedly consider it foolish and hysterical.

There was no one in the room. The only closet was a cretonne curtain tacked across one corner. It did not reach to the floor, and I assured myself that there were no feet showing under it. The only other hiding place was under the high iron bed, and from my position at the door I could see that there was nothing but dust there.

I turned and fled and got all the way down to the kitchen door before I took time to stop and think. I decided then to go to Allan, because I felt sure, somehow, that Jennie and Mr. Keith would merely laugh at me.

I found Allan in the study, still sitting before the fire and still drinking. I did not get a chance to more than open my mouth before he said curtly, "Run along, Calisthenics. I'm not taking you to the movies. I'm not in the mood."

I was instantly furious and I began, "I didn't come here—"

"I know, I know," he interrupted impatiently. "But get out, just the same. I can't be bothered with you."

I turned abruptly and went out. I was boiling with rage, and I did not trust myself to go to the kitchen, where I heard Jennie and Mr. Keith talking together. I went into the dining room and sat down at the table.

I didn't know what to do. I felt that I simply couldn't go up to my haunted room again, and I began to wish that Detective Hatton, or even Bill, would show up. But there was no sign of either.

Ross walked into the room just then and raised an amused eyebrow. "Well, well, fancy meeting you here. What is it—a rendezvous?"

"No, sir," I said. "It's the dining room."

He drew out a chair and sat down beside me.

I stood up because I realized that I had no business to be there, anyway, but he pulled me down again. "Come, now, don't run away; stay here and talk to me. I've nothing to do but be miserable. Can't you cheer me up with the story of your life, or something?"

"I'm saving it for the newspapers," I said briefly.

He gave me a charming little smile and said, "I didn't intend to buy it. In fact, I haven't any money at all. I started out tonight to get away from all this gloom and found that I didn't even have the price of a soda."

"Too bad," I said flatly. I didn't want to fool around with Ross. I knew he was merely trying to pick up some fun, and I knew, too, that if I told him about the rocking chair he'd want to go straight up to my room to investigate.

I murmured a firm apology and left him there, looking rather gloomy. I was pretty sure that I had been his last chance for any sort of an evening.

I went slowly upstairs, and when I reached the third floor I heard the rocker creaking. I stood out in the hall, with my teeth beginning to chatter, and wondered whether to dash into my room and catch the elusive occupant of that chair, or dash downstairs and arouse the household.

The thought of Mr. Keith's impervious superiority got the better of me at last, and I rushed into my room.

It was only Franny, after all. She looked up at me and said, "I thought you'd never come."

"But—but how long have you been here?" I stammered.

"I came straight up after dinner."

After dinner l I drew a quick breath and said, "You went away once though."

She said, "No. I've been here all the time."

My legs began to feel wobbly, and I sat down on the bed. "Miss Franny, I came up once before, and you were not here."

She dropped her eyes and looked faintly uncomfortable. "I've been here all the time," she insisted, "but I might have fallen asleep for a few minutes."

"I suppose you become invisible when you fall asleep."

She laughed. "Silly girl. The idea—such nonsense!"

"Well, that's what you implied."

She began to show signs of losing her temper. "I don't know what you're talking about," she said crossly. "As a matter of fact, I sometimes walk in my sleep."

I nearly laughed aloud at that. I knew that even if she had walked in her sleep I must have seen her in the hall or coming out of my room, since the rocker would continue to sway for only a matter of seconds after she left it.

"Well, perhaps that's what happened," I said mildly. "Do you think you walked in your sleep tonight?"

She pretended to concentrate for a moment, and then she slowly nodded her head. "Do you know, I believe I did."

"Where do you suppose you walked to?" I asked, watching her.

"I might have gone upstairs to the top floor. I was probably looking for my—" Her voice trailed into silence, and I prompted anxiously: "What were you looking for?"

"Oh, nothing," she snapped impatiently. "Nothing nothing at all," and she began to rock furiously.

I shrugged and resentfully decided that she was no longer my responsibility. I felt that she should be under the care of a doctor, but I had twice tried to tell Allan about it, and I didn't see why I should bother any further.

I glanced at Franny and felt sudden pity for her. She looked desperately tired, and she seemed to be dropping off to sleep. I got up and tried to persuade her to lie down on the bed for a while.

She was reluctant, but she agreed at last, on condition that I would hold the rocking chair for her.

She dropped off to sleep almost as her head touched the pillow, and I was sitting there, looking at her, when there was a knock on the door.

I flew over and pulled it open a crack, and Mr. Keith said, "You are wanted on the telephone, Ellen."

I stared at him for a moment before I realized that it must be Selma. He was already on his way downstairs before I had collected myself sufficiently to ask if the person had given a name.

"It is a Miss Jane Schmaltz," said Mr. Keith.

It was quite clear that he didn't believe it, and I felt sure that he must know Selma's voice on the phone. I cursed her for an utter fool as I made my way down the stairs.

I lifted the phone, said, "Hello," and it was my final word—much to Jennie's disappointment, I think.

Selma said, "Listen, Callie, get those letters and let me have them by tomorrow. It's coming up tomorrow, you know, and I'll give you my mink coat as well as the roadster. Phone me the minute you have them, and I'll make all arrangements." She cut the connection with a bang that hurt my ear, and I stared at the blank phone for an instant and then put it down.

Apparently she had not heard about George, but I wasn't thinking about that so much as about the mink coat. It was a beauty!

Jennie asked curiously, "Who was it?"

I sat down at the kitchen table. "Just a girl friend name of Schmaltz."

"An old friend?"

"Yes and no," I said.

"Well—" She hesitated, trying to think of some way in which she could pry loose the life history of Jane Schmaltz.

Mr. Keith was not interested in our petty woman's affairs. "There's an element of danger in that gun lying around somewhere. I am going to find it."

"Where?" Jennie asked.

"If I knew where," he said, to Jennie's confusion, "there would be no necessity for me to search. I shall start on this floor and go through it thoroughly."

"Well—I don't know," Jennie murmured uneasily. "I think it's better to leave that to them that are paid for it."

He shook his head. "I am going to find that gun. I shall feel a lot safer once it is in proper hands."

Bill walked into the kitchen, and I wondered if he were going to ask me to go to the movies. But it wasn't that. It seemed that Detective Hatton wanted to see me in the sitting room.

I went along, feeling a bit apprehensive, and as soon as I stepped into the sitting room Detective Hatton thrust his opened hand under my eyes and asked, "Ever seen these before?"

I looked down and saw a collection of burnt matches lying on his palm.

"No," I said innocently. "I mean, I've seen burnt matches before, of course, but I can't say I've seen those."

"You should have seen them," he said, watching my face.

I backed away a step and asked warily, "Why?"

"They were scattered all over the drawing-room floor. I found them yesterday morning."

I tried to keep my face blank as I realized that these were the matches I had dropped while I was trying to light my way through to the study on Sunday night. "I didn't see them," I said and hoped that my voice was quite steady.

"But you were supposed to have cleaned that room before we arrived."

I said, "Yes, but I didn't do the floor—I only dusted."

He seemed dissatisfied. "If they were there before you cleaned the room you should have seen them, whether you did the floor or not. Any woman would notice a thing like that."

I shook my head helplessly. I hadn't noticed them, and yet of course they must have been there, since I had dropped them the night before.

Detective Hatton dismissed me, and I went back to the kitchen, feeling distinctly uneasy. Jennie and Mr. Keith had gone upstairs, and after a moment's indecision I followed them.

The third floor was in darkness, and I groped my way along the hall, cursing Jennie's thriftiness and shivering with nervousness.

I had nearly reached my door when a sound from behind me caused me to look fearfully over my shoulder.

I could just make out a figure that looked like Franny, slowly mounting the stairs to the top story.

CHAPTER TWELVE

For a minute or two as I stood there, I felt quite homeless. I was afraid to go into my room, where a rocking chair swayed itself, and I was terrified of that dark fourth floor, where, for all I knew, Franny was even now sticking straws in her hair.

In the end I followed her. She seemed to have become more or less my responsibility, and I knew that I ought to find her and bring her down again.

I climbed the stairs quietly. It was very dark, but I was in time to see the vague outlines of Franny's figure disappearing into one of the front rooms. I went in after her and paused by the door, straining my eyes into the darkness. As far as I could make out, she seemed to be leaning out one of the opened windows, with her arms raised up toward the roof. My mind clicked back to the Sunday of my arrival, and I was certain that it had been Franny I had seen then leaning out the fourth-floor window, and with her arms raised to the roof, just as she was now.

She seemed not to have heard me, and I kept very still. I thought that if I had something tangible to report to Allan I might force him to have her put under medical care.

She presently withdrew from the window, and I backed stealthily out into the hall again. It was still raining, and I could see her mopping at her wet hair. She was muttering to herself, but I could not separate any words.

She came out of the room after a while, and I flattened myself against the wall. She passed quite close to me, clicked her tongue in evident annoyance and groped her way into another room. I crept to the door and peered in, and I could see her standing there, and suddenly, in a loud whisper, she said, "Alice! Are you here?"

Blank silence followed this, and then she turned and came back into the hall. I stopped breathing and heard her grope her way to the stairs and start down. I followed cautiously and was hardly surprised when she went into my room and I heard the rhythmic squeak of the rocker.

My knees were wobbly and I was perspiring freely, and after a moment's indecision I decided that what I needed was a hot bath. I went into the bathroom and had the tub almost filled, when Jennie knocked on the door. I let her in, and she asked if she might brush her teeth before I started my bath. I nodded, and she took possession and started a fairly amiable lecture on the dangers of taking too many hot baths. "It's very weakening, you know. I don't wonder you fainted today. And then, of course, Mr. Allan blames it all on me and makes out I've been working you too hard."

"Oh, don't worry about that," I said carelessly. "I told him it wasn't your fault."

"Did you *really?*" she asked in a pleased voice. "Well, I *am* glad. I hate to be blamed for something that isn't my fault."

I sat on the edge of the bathtub and lit a cigarette and wished that she would go.

But it began to be obvious that she was settling down for a good gossip. She glanced at me and said, "Mercy! Do you have to smoke in the bathroom too?"

I said absently, "Doctor's orders," and had to spend five minutes clearing it up.

I could not offer any gossip, so I smoked five cigarettes while she gave me some instead. It seemed that Franny had nearly died of grief and jealousy when Hattie and George were married, and Jennie doubted that she had been right in the head since that time. Hattie had been George's secretary—before he lost his job—and was scornfully described as a cheapskate. Before her advent Franny and George had been very companionable and had gone around together.

"Gone around?" I repeated.

Jennie said, "I mean, they went to church together and to the movies, and they always took a Sunday afternoon drive. But that Hattie one stopped all that. She wouldn't let them go out together, and even when she didn't want to go with Mr. George herself, she wouldn't hear of him going anywhere with Miss Franny."

"What about Hattie and Oliver?" I asked bluntly.

But for some reason—I suspected loyalty to her own kind—she would not discuss it. She merely said, "What do you mean?" and then turned the tap on hard so that she could not hear any more.

I let it go, and when she turned the tap off she told me something of Ross. It seemed that he just turned up and foisted himself on Allan every now and then. He was an insurance salesman and did very well with it, but he was extravagant and lived beyond his means, and so he fell back on Allan's bounty when he was broke. He had introduced Selma to Allan—and speaking of Selma, she was a shocking wife, always inviting men friends for the weekend. But Mr. Allan had never said a word about it, and when the separation came Franny and George had been quite horrified. They had sent the minister, Mr. Evans, to talk to Mr. Allan, but Mr. Allan refused to listen.

At this point Jennie hung her damp washcloth on the towel rack and yawned. I disposed of my fifth cigarette and asked her if she knew who Alice was.

"Oh yes," Jennie said, yawning again. "Alice was George's and Franny's younger sister. She died when she was sixteen."

Left to myself, I climbed into my bath and wondered if my hair was on end, because that was the way I felt. I thought of Franny standing in that dark room and calling to a sister who had been dead these many years.

I gave myself a mental shake and reflected that, anyway, there had been no ghostly answering voice. I further requested myself to remember that Franny was unbalanced.

I got out of the bath, dried myself and went to my room. Franny was asleep in the rocker, her head fallen awkwardly to one side and her mouth open. She was snoring slightly.

I was pretty sure she would awake with a crick in her neck, but I did not like to disturb her, so I stretched out on my bed and began to make plans for a further search for the letters. The roadster and the mink coat were too much for me, and anyway, Allan had been abominably rude. Of course he could always make trouble for me with Detective Hatton, but on the other hand that would mean changing his own story, which might get him into a mess, too.

I glanced at the clock and saw that it was ten past ten. I wanted to search Allan's bedroom, and I decided wearily that I'd better go at once, before he took himself to bed.

I got up, and after a moment's hesitation I woke Franny and told her to lie down on the bed for a while. She agreed, rubbing gingerly at her neck, but insisted that I hold the rocker for her. "You must not leave the room," she said anxiously. "They'll get me if you do."

I felt my hair rising again and asked, "What do you mean? Who will get you?"

She eyed me squarely. "They got George, didn't they? And now they're after me. But I'm going to be careful."

"Miss Franny," I said earnestly, "if you know who killed your brother you simply must tell the police."

She became vague again immediately and murmured that she didn't know, really, and that she'd tell very soon, anyhow. Her "they" made me curious, and I asked if it were more than one person, but she said no, only one, and then shut up like a clam. .

I watched her until she fell asleep, and then I put on my robe and went downstairs. I had made up my mind to tell someone about her condition, and I hoped to run into either Detective Hatton or Bill. I went on down to the ground floor with this in mind, but I saw no one except Allan, who had gone to sleep in front of the dead fire in the study. I made no attempt to rouse him. I was sure that he was in a drunken stupor and would be no use to me in any case.

I went back to the front hall and stood there, hesitating. Somehow I did not want to tell any other member of the household about Franny. Any one of them could have killed George, and if I happened to pick that one, both Franny and I might be in active danger.

In the midst of my indecision Hattie walked through the front door. I had barely time to slip down the corridor, and she did not see me, but I managed a good look at her. She was crying openly, with the tears making ugly streaks through her makeup, but I thought she seemed angry too.

I went up the back stairs and decided to give my information to Detective Hatton as soon as I saw him in the morning.

On the second floor Selma's mink coat occupied my mind again, and I cautiously made my way to Allan's room. I slipped in, closed the door and switched on the light. I felt perfectly safe. Allan was out cold, and I did not suppose that anyone else would have any business in his bedroom at that hour.

I went through the desk first and drew an absolute blank. I was still standing in front of it, with a small leather memorandum book that I had picked up clutched in my hand, when I heard cautious footsteps directly outside the door.

I raised my head, and at the same time the door swung slowly inward.

CHAPTER THIRTEEN

I DROPPED the little notebook into my pocket and flew into the clothes closet as someone quietly opened the bedroom door and cautiously closed it again. There was very little sound after that, and I felt sure it could not be Allan; whoever had come into the bedroom was being much too careful.

I had left the closet door open about an inch, but it was some time before the intruder came into my line of vision, and when at last he did I recognized Ross. He was silently and methodically going through the bureau drawers.

Apparently he did not find what he was looking for, and after he had finished with the bureau he frowned, shook his head and moved off to another part of the room.

After a while I stopped being afraid and began to get bored and irritable. I wished that Ross would finish his search and go, and it seemed to me that Allan must be a heel, keeping things that belonged to other people, so that he could have the whip hand.

It took Ross well over half an hour to go through the room, and then he left as quietly as he had come. I emerged from the closet, and after stretching my cramped limbs tried to think where I was up to. I remembered, after a moment, that I had finished the desk, so I started on the bureau.

But there was to be no peace. Someone came up the stairs, and I could hear the footsteps heading in my direction. I retired to the closet again, and immediately afterward the bedroom door opened and then closed firmly, and not at all carefully.

I knew it was Allan, even before I saw him, and I had time only for a moment of panic before he came straight to the closet, threw open the door and started to hang up his coat.

I was in full view, and there was nothing I could do but stand there and stare back at him wildly. It was quite clear that he was far from being in a drunken stupor.

I could not think of any word in the English language that seemed appropriate, so I fished a cigarette from my pocket and lit it.

He looked me over for a moment and then asked courteously, "Visiting?"

I think in my confusion I may have nodded.

"Shall I bring a chair in here for you, or would you prefer to sit out in the room where there is more air?" he asked, still polite.

I walked out into the room then and made straight for the door, but I wasn't much surprised when it did not work. He got there before me and turned the key in the lock. "I would not have you leave me with so much still unexplained between us."

I sat down in an armchair and went on with my smoking. Allan lighted his pipe, threw himself onto the bed and gave a certain amount of thoughtful attention to the ceiling.

"You're not drunk any more, are you?" I said, starting the conversational ball rolling.

"No. I was as drunk as I ever get this afternoon, but it's worn off."

"Fancy that!" I said brightly. "I know a man who was drunk for three weeks by the clock."

He said, "Fancy that! Have you found those letters yet?"

"Why, no," I murmured and felt myself blushing.

"Nor have I, but I'd like to turn them up. I suggest that you finish your search of this room before you go."

"Oh no, I don't think I'll bother looking any more," I said hastily over a mental picture of myself finding the letters and being forced to hand them over to Allan along with any chance for the roadster and the mink coat. "I'm not so anxious to find them now, anyway."

"Perhaps not. But I don't intend that you shall leave here until you have finished your search."

I settled myself more comfortably into the chair. "That's quite all right. I've no place to go, anyway."

He glanced at me and asked, "Aren't you interested in getting any sleep tonight?"

"I can sleep in this chair," I said agreeably. "It's more comfortable than that housemaid's bed you provide upstairs."

"Have you considered the safety angle?" he asked, and I thought, with a faint uneasiness, that he was beginning to get nasty. "I might be the most dangerous person in the house."

"Might you?" I said, yawning.

He banged his pipe down on the table and, heaving himself off the bed, advanced on me with an expression that sent my heart into my mouth.

He put a firm hand on my arm and jerked me to my feet. His voice was low, but it had me scared. "Now search this room, and search it quickly—and don't try to put anything over on me, you damned little crook, because you're going to be searched yourself, thoroughly, before you leave, if you don't produce the letters."

He dropped my arm, and I began to search in a hurry, while he went back to the bed and picked up his pipe again.

I knew that I was being bullied and had not even tried to fight back, and what could he do, anyway, if I defied him? But I went on searching on the off chance that he might, after all, be the fiend who had killed poor George.

I found the letters after a while. They were in a small cabinet with a lot of bills and various papers of that sort.

I turned toward the bed, prepared to hand them over with regret, and then I stopped. Allan was lying quite still, and his eyes were closed. I considered him for a while, and then, experimentally, I walked to the door. He did not move, and I stood there, hesitating. I was sure that if I turned the lock the small sound would wake him, and after a moment's thought I knelt down and pushed the letters under the bottom of the door out into the hall. I stood up and turned the lock carelessly and then waited, but apparently he slept on.

I went up to my room with the letters clutched in my hand and feeling so desperately tired that I was determined to push Franny over and sleep beside her.

But Franny was back in the rocker and deeply offended with me. "It's very unkind and thoughtless of you, Ellen, to leave me all the time when you know I'm in such danger."

I was trying to find a hiding place for my letters, and I asked absently, "Are you in danger, Miss Franny?"

"I've told you a hundred times that I am," she said furiously. "I'm in danger of my life."

"But why don't you tell the police?" I protested. "They ought to know, and they could look after you."

"I can't—I don't want to. I have a *reason* for not telling them."

"Then tell me," I said persuasively, "so that I'll know how to protect you."

"No, no. You mustn't bother me. I can't tell anyone. You can protect me if you'll only stay with me." She began to rock herself, with her lips folded into an obstinate line.

I knew it was useless to press her, and I thought gloomily that if there were any truth in what she said the murderer might get desperate after a while and simply lump Franny and me together in one killing.

The thought frightened me, and I sat down on the side of the bed and read Selma's letters in an effort to calm myself. There were only two, both addressed to Dick, and Selma had certainly gone to town. I noticed that they had not been posted, which was a pity, because Dick would certainly have enjoyed them. I hid them under a slip in the bureau drawer, because I was too tired to think of a smarter place.

I asked Franny if she wanted to lie on the bed, but she said no sulkily. "I'll have to stay awake to be sure that you don't leave me again."

I threw myself onto the bed without removing my robe or turning out the light and then found that something was pressing into my side uncomfortably.

It turned out to be the little memorandum book that I had jammed into my pocket when Ross had frightened me into the closet.

I rifled through its pages idly and accompanied always by a sense of guilt. After all, the book belonged to Allan, and although it was not a diary, it was filled with things like "have car greased" and "get watch repaired."

And then I ran across "must talk to George by the fourteenth"!

CHAPTER FOURTEEN

I READ the thing over three times and then lay there, thinking about it in a tired, confused sort of way. Had Allan seen George by the fourteenth? And if so, did he shoot him? But then, Allan had gone upstairs before I did on Sunday night. On the other hand, he might have shot George before he came to the study. I decided that if he had he must be a thoroughly cold proposition, because he had certainly showed no signs of fluster.

I passed out from pure exhaustion at that point, and I must have slept heavily, because when I opened my eyes the room was light and Franny had gone. Rain still dripped against the window, and when I turned my head I saw that Allan was standing in front of the bureau. He had the letters in his hand. I silently cursed myself for a fool, for not having hidden them better.

He glanced at me and saw that my eyes were open.

"Don't let me catch you looking for these letters again," he said by way of greeting. "They're going in a safe-deposit vault this morning."

I said, "Yes sir."

He went out, and I raised my head and looked at the clock. It was eight-thirty, and I jumped out of bed and began to dress in a hurry. I wondered what had happened to Jennie and refused to believe that she was letting me sleep out of the goodness of her heart.

When I got down to the kitchen Jennie let me know about it. "Well, you're a nice one, I must say. Were you waiting for someone to bring your breakfast up, or what? Here I tried to wake you, and I couldn't get a thing out of you. I even shook your shoulder, and you pushed me away without waking up."

I had no recollection of pushing her away. I said meekly, "So what did you do?"

"I went and told Mr. Allan, and he said don't bother because you were probably sleepy—joking, you see-—and I told him you might be ill, so he said he'd go up and have a look at you. Did he go up and look at you?"

I said, "Yes. Did you see Miss Barton?"

"Her?" said Jennie, surprised. "No. I haven't seen her this morning. But I have her tray ready here, and you're to take it up."

I tried to argue Jennie into letting Franny's tray wait for a while, because I knew how tired she was and how badly she needed sleep, but Jennie knew nothing about it, of course, and merely thought I was being lazy. She put the tray firmly into my hands, and I was obliged to march upstairs with it.

Franny did not answer my knock, and when I went in I found her sleeping soundly. I did not have the heart to wake her, so I backed out again and took the breakfast with me. I thought I might save a little labor by taking it in to Hattie, but it didn't work. She took one look at the tray after I had placed it on her bed and let out an indignant howl. "Take this away. This isn't mine; it's the sort of muck that Franny eats. You must have got the trays switched. And hurry—I want mine as soon as possible."

Jennie did a lot of fussing when Franny's tray was returned to her, but I stood my ground, and she gave in at last and handed me Hattie's breakfast.

I could hear Hattie talking to someone as I approached her door, and she said rather loudly and quite clearly, "I don't care what they say. I'm going to have things my way."

I knocked and went in to find Oliver standing there, cap in hand. Hattie had tied a blue ribbon around her head and looked foul. Almost automatically I went over and lowered the Venetian blinds to help her out, but she was not appreciative. She roared at me to raise them again, and then yelled at me to get out.

Oliver, who was passing the time by spinning his cap around on one finger, gave me a wink as I crossed the room on my way to the door, and unfortunately Hattie saw it. I eavesdropped outside the door and listened to Oliver getting it. She dressed him down thoroughly and ended by saying, "I won't have you making up to every cheap little flirt that comes along."

I had an impulse to go in and protest that, but Hattie had burst into noisy sobs, so I contented myself by shaking my head over her technique and walked away.

Jennie was just starting me in to work when Detective Hatton asked to have me produced. I answered the call with real pleasure and hoped that he would detain me until someone else had to do my work:

He received me in the sitting room and courteously gave me permission to smoke. I lit up, dropped the match happily into an ashtray and at the same time noticed an old black felt hat lying on the table. It was a lady's hat, wet and battered, and I recognized it in an instant as the one Selma had given me and which I had later thrown into the bushes in a temper.

Detective Hatton had been watching me, and he said at once, "You've seen that hat before?"

I prepared to lie and thought better of it; after all, it was nothing that mattered. I told him I had thrown it away because it was old and had got very wet.

He nodded and said, "Well, that clears that up. But how is it that the hat belonged to Mrs. Allan Barton?"

I wondered frantically how much Allan had told him and said idiotically, "How on earth did you know that ?"

"Jennie identified it," he explained impatiently.

"Oh yes, of course. Yes—Mrs. Barton gave it to me. I needed it for this—my work here, you understand, and I knew she was going to throw it away."

"I see," he said thoughtfully and looked at me for some time. "So you know Mrs. Barton quite well?"

"Oh yes. Best of friends," I murmured uneasily.

He let me go after that, and since I had not been with him for long and I figured that Jennie would not be gunning for me just yet, I sneaked upstairs to try and snatch a little extra sleep. I was tired enough and I felt that I really needed it.

I reached my room safely and flopped down on the bed, but although I was aching with weariness I found that I could not sleep.

I began to think about the fourth floor after a while and to wonder what business Franny had up there, outside of looking for her dead sister. The thing gave me goose flesh and fascinated me at the same time. I wanted to investigate the place by daylight, and after shivering over the thought for a few minutes I pulled myself off the bed and decided to go at once. At least I would be out of Jennie's way, since I felt sure that she would never think of looking up there for me.

I was none too soon, either. I had just reached the top of the stairs when I heard Jennie banging on the bathroom door and yelling, "Are you taking another bath in there?"

I made a face in her general direction and tiptoed across the dusty surface of the square hall. I found that two of the rooms were used for storage and were so crammed with cobwebby rubbish that it was almost impossible to get into them. The room into which Franny had first gone was at the front and had only an ancient green plush sofa by way of furnishing. I noticed that the window was still open, and rain was dripping onto the floor over the sill, so I closed it. I could not find anything of interest, so I went to the room where Franny had called to Alice.

There seemed to have been some attempt at furnishing this room. There was a bed, made up, but crumpled, and looking much the same as my own effort at bedmaking. There was also a rocking chair, but a larger and more elaborate edition than the one in my room. An old-fashioned bureau stood against the wall, and I went over and looked through the drawers. There was a quantity of yellowed, out-of-date underwear, artificial flowers, bits of lace and ribbons—things that had belonged to the dead Alice, I supposed.

A chill began to creep along my spine, and I felt the hair prickling on my scalp. I turned in a panic came face to face with the oil painting of a young girl and fled in utter defeat. Even my bedroom seemed suddenly full of horror, with the chair that rocked of itself and the print of an animal's paw when there were no animals.

I passed it by and went on downstairs. On the second floor I decided to show a little independence and do the bedrooms first, so I collected the various brooms and dusters and started in on the nearest room, which happened to be Ross's.

I began to mop the floor the way Jennie had showed me, but when I started to push the thing under the bed I was startled to discover that Ross was still in it. Further, he was awake and looking at me.

I stopped, abashed, but he said good-naturedly, "It's all right; don't mind me. I'm not paying any board, you know."

"I'm very sorry, sir," I said primly. "I didn't notice you. I thought you was a heap of clothes." I started to collect my tools, but he produced a package of cigarettes and turned on all his charm.

"Don't go. I wish you wouldn't. Have a cigarette with me, now that you know I'm not the laundry."

I never could resist a cigarette, so I took one and eased my aching bones into a chair.

"Now come on out from behind the bad grammar," he said, smiling at me, "and tell me how you got into this servant racket."

"I'm an actress. I am determined to succeed, but these days you need a private income while you're waiting to be discovered, so I do this sort of thing for a couple of months every now and then, and that enables me to go on for a while."

He said, "Good stuff, kid. I guess you'll succeed all right," and chuckled to himself for a while. I didn't know whether he believed me or not.

"Then why are you so standoffish?" he asked presently. "Why don't you come over and sit on the side of the bed?"

I said, "Oh, no indeed. I'm not that type at all."

"Listen," said Ross, but I didn't listen, because Allan walked into the room at that moment, and I was thrown into utter confusion. I jumped up, threw my cigarette onto the floor, crushed it out with my foot and then picked up the butt and stood with it in my fingers, looking at him.

He glanced at me and said, "Get out, and don't let me catch you wasting your time like this again."

I walked out with some of the brooms under my arm and stood in the hall, muttering. I thought of several stinging things that I could have said to Allan and had half a mind to go back and say them. While I hesitated Detective Hatton came along and hailed me.

"Miss Drake, I want to have a talk with you. Miss Barton tells me she met you coming up the stairs on Sunday night long after your statement had you in bed."

CHAPTER FIFTEEN

I AUTOMATICALLY tried to register amazement, while my mind darted about frantically. I had forgotten about having met Franny in the upper hall, and I was quite unprepared with an explanation of any sort.

"Evidently," said Detective Hatton, "you went downstairs again for some reason. Do you mind telling me why? And what you did and whom you saw?"

It was clear that he was not in any mood to be put off with foolishness, and I allowed the poor attempt at amazement to fade from my face. But what could I say? Had Allan been approached? Probably not, since it was quite possible that Franny had not been there when he went up.

Detective Hatton watched me squirm for a moment and then said persuasively, "Why not tell the truth?"

I threw up my head, bit my lip and said, "I will!" and knew that the words were sheer hypocrisy. I had no intention whatever of telling the truth.

I began to speak and was utterly appalled to hear myself tell the man that Allan and I were secret lovers. I asked him, with a touch of wistfulness, not to give us away and explained that we had arranged a late meeting in the study, because I was not the type to go to a man's bedroom or allow him to come to mine. I added that we had seen no one downstairs and had returned to our rooms after a short talk, and I had met Franny at the head of the stairs.

"You are quite sure that you saw no one else?" he asked quietly.

After a moment's hesitation I remembered having seen George sitting in the dining room, but I did not mention Hattie or Oliver.

He said, "Thank you," and turned away abruptly, and I saw him heading straight for Allan's bedroom. I knew he was seeking immediate confirmation of my tale, but I had the jump on him, since I knew where Allan was. I made a dive for Ross's bedroom, burst in without knocking and banged the door shut behind me.

Allan was sitting in an armchair, and Ross was standing in front of the bureau in his underwear. They both turned to stare at me, and then Ross said with dignity, "Excuse me," and disappeared into the connecting bathroom.

I turned to Allan and said in a hoarse, hurried whisper, "Mr. Barton— I've put my foot in it."

"You astonish me," he said with chilly sarcasm. "What is it now?"

Ross reentered, respectably clad in a dressing gown, and I glanced at him, hesitating. At the same moment I heard footsteps approaching the door, so I flew over beside Allan and whispered the frightful thing into his ear. I had just finished when there was a peremptory knock on the door, and with a little gasp I turned and fled into the bathroom. I knew that it opened into Franny's room on the other side and offered a safe escape. I had one last fleeting look at Allan's face, and its expression warned me that I had better keep well out of his way for some time to come.

I had time to recognize Detective Hatton's voice in the room behind me before I slipped through Franny's room and out into the hall. I found myself wondering irrelevantly how it was possible for Franny and Ross to share a bathroom.

I went on down to the kitchen, found it deserted and immediately started scrubbing one of the tables with a scrubbing brush. I thought it might go down well with Jennie.

However, the thing worked in reverse. Jennie presently appeared and instantly flew into a rage. "I'll have you know my kitchen is kept spotlessly clean," she yelled furiously. "If you'd get busy on your own work, instead of insulting other people, you pert minx—"

I dropped the brush and tried to soothe her. I explained that her table was, and always had been, spotless, that I had no idea of cleaning it, but was merely trying to kill an ant. Elaborating, I added that in a kitchen as clean as Jennie's, it could not, of course, have been an ant and was probably a spot in front of my eye; the chances were that I needed glasses.

Jennie grunted and sent me in to set the table.

I spent the afternoon in trying to get my housework done and keep out of Allan's way at the same time. I managed to get up to my room at about five o'clock, where I fell onto the bed in utter exhaustion. I felt dusty and grubby, and my beautiful costume was dirty and crumpled.

I got into a hot bath after a while and took the apron in with me and washed it. The water was so soapy and grimy after I had finished that I had to run another complete tubful to rinse off both myself and the apron.

Back in my room, I hung the apron over the rocking chair and climbed back into bed.

It did not last long, of course. Mr. Keith presently came knocking at the door with the intelligence that I was wanted by Jennie in the kitchen, and I actually said, "Yes sir," to him.

My apron was not dry, of course, so I had to go down without it. I set the table but tried to beg off service in the dining room. "You see," I explained with a touch of triumph, "I have no apron."

Jennie said, "Heavenly days, girl, the house is full of aprons," and produced one of her own—a great, starched, ugly thing that went around me twice. She tied me firmly into it and sent me along to the dining room with Mr. Keith.

They were all there. Franny looked a bit more spruce in a black dress with a touch of jet and her hair piled high on her head. Hattie wore her new weeds, up to and including the hat, with its yards of black veiling. She was obviously and inexpertly trying to pick up Ross—and failing badly. What Allan was doing I did not know, because I never looked at him once; he was merely a blur to me. I was sure that if he caught my eye I would get a mental thrashing with the promise of worse to come.

Hattie, possibly goaded by Ross's indifference, presently made an hysterical announcement to the effect that she was going into New York on the following day, directly after the funeral, and would stay there until the thing was cleared up.

Nobody said anything for a moment, while Hattie looked around expectantly, and then Franny expressed her opinion in one contemptuous word.

"Shocking!" said Franny.

Hattie turned on her and shrilled angrily, "What do you mean, 'shocking'?"

"George hardly cold," Franny said primly without lifting her eyes from her plate, "and you want to go carousing in New York."

"Carousing!" Hattie shrieked. "How dare you! I want to hide my grief. I—"

Allan's voice suddenly cut across her hysteria. "Have you any money with which to stay in New York, Hattie?"

After a moment's silence she said, staring at him, "You know good and well that I haven't."

"Then I'm afraid that you won't be able to go," Allan said courteously.

"Do you mean to say that you are going to withhold the money?" she asked, breathing heavily.

"What money?" said Allan.

Hattie took a couple of strangling breaths and waited for Mr. Keith and me to get out of the room. We both lingered in the service pantry, he with his ear to the door, and I busy with the task of changing from one dessert to another the maraschino cherries with which they were topped.

I missed something that Hattie said, and then I heard Allan's voice quite clearly. "You know perfectly well, Hattie, that George has had no money for years, so that anything I don't give you can hardly be termed 'withheld.' "

There was quiet for the rest of the meal after that.

When we had finished our own dinner I stayed close to Jennie, working almost as hard as she was, while Mr. Keith and Oliver had a fight. It was no brawl, of course, with Mr. Keith on one end of it, and naturally no vulgar blows were exchanged.

Mr. Keith started it by saying in a quiet, conversational sort of voice that in his opinion Oliver should resign his post as chauffeur and leave at once.

Oliver had just taken out his pipe to join Mr. Keith in their usual after-dinner smoke, while we women worked, and he stopped with the lighted match halfway to the bowl and stared. The stare lasted until the match burned his fingers, when he swore and demanded, "What the devil do you mean?"

"To put it a little more plainly," said Mr. Keith, who had put it quite plainly enough, "I think that you should leave now—immediately."

"I don't give a goddam what you think," Oliver said angrily. "Have you gone bughouse, or what?"

"It is because of Mrs. Barton, Mrs. *Hattie* Barton," said Mr. Keith, bringing the thing out into the open.

Oliver pushed back his chair noisily and began to pace the kitchen furiously. "Have you the crust to try and tell me I got to give up a good job because that fat, bleached broad takes a fancy to me?"

Jennie clicked her tongue and shook her head several times. Mr. Keith said smoothly, "Naturally, such a thing would never have been expected of you if you had kept her in her place. But you did not. You cooperated—for the monetary gain, I dare say—with the result that it is now imperative that you leave."

"What the hell difference would it make if I did go?" Oliver demanded hotly. "Are you tryin' to tell me that nosy little jerk Hatton would find out about it any easier if I stayed?"

"Certainly," said Mr. Keith. "Particularly since you still spend a good deal of time each morning up in her room."

"Well, waddamy supposed to do? Tell her to go tie a can to herself when she sends for me? She gives me instructions for the day every morning. You want me to tell her to quit stallin' and be her age? What the hell! I'm stayin' here, see? And you can tell that flatfoot all about it. I'm still not leavin'."

Mr. Keith knocked his pipe out and said, "I shall not inform on you." He gave Oliver an odd glance and added, "It would not be necessary, even if I wanted to." Oliver said, "Ah, nuts!" and banged out the back door.

Jennie turned around from the sink, shaking her head and saying, "Tch, tch." I found myself doing the same, probably with some vague idea of keeping in well with them. But Mr. Keith looked at me stonily, and I realized that I was wrong again. I should, of course, have closed my ears and not listened to any of it.

I stuck around with the Keiths and went up to bed when they did at a little before nine. I found Franny already there, silently rocking herself, and she gave me only a brief, dull glance.

I got undressed and then took my uniform into the bathroom. I had made up my mind to wash it, and as far as I could see, the easiest method was simply to give it a bath, as the hand basin seemed too small.

Jennie banged on the door when I was half finished and commanded me to come out at once, as this was Mr. Keith's bath night, and I was having the effrontery to hold him up. When I came out at last Jennie went in at once on a tour of inspection. I left her there, muttering her dissatisfaction.

Somewhat to my surprise Franny had gone when I returned to my room. I gave the rocking chair a suspicious scrutiny, but it was quite still. I hung up my uniform to dry and got into bed without much hope of being able to sleep, but I dropped off almost immediately with the light full on. I remember worrying a little, Jennie-fashion, about wasting the electricity when I felt myself getting drowsy.

I slept restlessly and woke after a while to find the room in darkness. I could hear the sway and creak of the rocking chair, and I raised my head and could just distinguish the huddled shape that sat in it.

"Is that you, Miss Franny?" I asked.

She said, "Yes," and added in a dead, hopeless voice, "I am waiting for the end. It will be tonight."

CHAPTER SIXTEEN

MY TEETH began to chatter, and I felt my heart thudding uncomfortably. I got out of bed and switched on the light. "What do you mean, Miss Franny?" I asked in a scared voice. "What—what are you talking about?"

She continued to rock slowly, her face old and dreadfully tired. "Go back to bed," she said dully. "You can't help me. Nobody can."

"But look," I said desperately, "you simply must tell the police what you know—or tell Allan, or somebody. Then you can get police protection."

"I won't tell," she said monotonously, "and I won't have police protection."

"But for heaven's sake, why?"

She said obscurely, "One good turn deserves another. You see, it's because of Alice—and I may be wrong."

I didn't see, but I realized that it was no use talking to her; she was certainly potty and getting rapidly worse. She ought to be in a hospital, I thought, and was determined to have something arranged for her first thing in the morning. In the meantime I felt that I should stay awake and watch her.

I perched myself uneasily on the side of the bed and wondered how I was going to pass the night away. It was only twelve o'clock, and I had no book. I began to think that I ought to try and get her taken away at once, but I did not know whom I could approach. Hattie would certainly tell me to go to hell. Ross would ask me to come in and have a drink, and I was afraid to go near Allan. I was sure that when he caught up with me I would get a word beating that I wouldn't forget in a hurry. Mr. Keith would have done very well, but I was too much of a coward to break into the midnight slumbers of Jennie and Mr. Keith; nothing short of a fire would have excused it. I decided to let it go and returned to my original plan of arranging everything in the morning.

Franny made a restless movement and said suddenly, "I have a fearful headache."

"You'd better lie on the bed," I said gently.

"No, no, I won't lie down. But if I could have two aspirin tablets?"

I had none and went to the bathroom, where a careful search failed to show any. I returned to Franny and asked her where they were to be found.

"In my room in the top drawer of the bureau," she said, pressing her hands against her temples.

"I'll go down and get them."

"Don't be long," she said wearily. "What's the use, anyway?"

I hurried downstairs with my spine creeping. The hall on the second floor was still lighted, and I looked carefully up and down before I stepped quietly across and into Franny's room. I was startled to find that the light was on, and an instant later I saw Ross. He had his back to me and was carefully searching one of the bureau drawers. He did not turn around and apparently had not heard me, so I backed out into the hall again. I stood there for a while, wondering what on earth he was trying to find that could conceivably be hidden either in Allan's room or Franny's.

There was a bathroom at the end of the hall, and after a moment's indecision I went quietly along to see if I could find aspirin there. I crept past Allan's door in fear and trembling and finally gained the bathroom without mishap. I found a bottle of aspirin tablets in the medicine cabinet and turned to leave with a sigh of relief, and at the same time the door was pushed inward, and an instant later Allan was in the bathroom with me.

He gave a startled jump, and I gasped, and then he turned and firmly closed the door. "Might as well thrash it out here as anywhere else, since you're so determinedly not the type to be caught in a man's bedroom."

I swallowed a mouthful of air and said hurriedly, "Mr. Barton, Miss Franny is not—"

"Don't try to change the subject," he said abruptly. "I'm glad to have met up with you. I couldn't move without stumbling over you for a while, but today there hasn't been a sign of you. If I didn't know you so well I'd think you had a guilty conscience. Now there are one or two things that will have to be settled between us, since you so naively announced to the world at large that we are lovers."

"Detective Hatton isn't the world at large," I said weakly. My legs were wobbling, but I felt that the only available seat was unsuited to what dignity I had left.

"If you interrupt again," he said rudely, "I'll muzzle you. As I was saying, since you have announced to the world at large that we are lovers, Selma won't be so desperate to get those letters; she can practically name her own alimony. You will be given that vulgar roadster, and I find a certain amount of satisfaction in believing that your parents will not allow you to keep it."

"My parents!" I muttered hollowly. "What—what do you know about my parents?"

"Naturally I checked up on you," he said impatiently. "You surely don't suppose I'd allow you to stay here—and even protect you—if I didn't know who you were?"

"Are you gong to tell them where I am?" I asked, on the verge of tears.

"No, I'm not. They are decent, charming people and don't deserve all that worry and unhappiness. I'm only sorry that they should have been so unfortunate in their only child."

I had known, of course, that when he got me it was going to be pretty bad, but I would never have thought that he could make me feel so utterly and devastatingly ashamed of myself and sorry for my parents. I dropped my head a little and stared at the floor, trying painfully and vainly to think of some way in which I could justify myself.

"There have been reporters all over the place," he went on after a moment, "and so far Keith has kept them away from us. But Detective Hatton gives them what news he can, and although he promised to keep your juicy little bit of secret I think it won't be long before it will prove too much for him."

I raised my head then and said simply, "My God!"

He shrugged. "I was forced to protect myself as far as I could, so I told him that you were violently in love with me and I was finding it very difficult to get rid of you."

I flew into a temper, and while I was struggling for speech he smiled for the first time. "Count ten," he suggested.

I tried to slap his face then, but he caught my arm in mid-passage. "You've done that once too often already. It's both stupid and defeatist."

"I agree with you," I said bitterly. "It's a thing I never did in my life until I came to this madhouse."

He dropped my arm. "Why don't you go back to bed?" he asked in a bored voice. "What the hell are you doing in this bathroom, anyway?"

"It's nothing to you, of course," I said coldly, "but I was getting aspirin for Miss Barton, who has taken to spending all her nights in my room. She's gone completely loopy now, and it's given her a headache." I pushed past him and added, "She's not the only cracked member of your family, either. Your brother Ross is searching Franny's room right now, and he searched yours yesterday."

"Miss Franny and Mr. Ross to you," Allan called after me.

I ignored him and went on up the stairs. When I got to the top I stopped and listened and thought I heard him walk down to Franny's room. I wondered a little why I had told on Ross and was faintly sorry about it.

Franny was still in the rocking chair, so I fed her the aspirins and again offered her my bed, but she shook her head and said that she did not want to be lying down when it happened.

"It!" I repeated, my voice sharpened by fear and exasperation. "What? Can't you tell me?"

She shook her head again and asked me to turn out the light. I stood looking at her until she snapped impatiently, "Come, girl, turn out the light. It hurts my eyes." She closed them and added fretfully, "I don't quite believe it myself. I don't really know. Hattie lied when she said George told me; he *didn't*. I'm just guessing, but I'm a good guesser." Her voice trailed off.

I turned the light out and sat down uneasily on the side of the bed, but after several minutes' thought I came to the conclusion that Franny was merely being dramatic and probably didn't know anything at all.

I lay down at last and was almost asleep, when Franny spoke suddenly into the darkness.

"You'll be good to Alice for me, won't you?"

I gasped and my flesh rose in goose pimples. I got off the bed and then stopped, with my eyes straining toward the door. I was sure that I had heard a faint noise from the hall, and the door seemed to be open a little wider than we were ordinarily obliged to leave it. Every faculty I possessed was strained to the utmost, yet for a moment I could hear nothing but the incessant creaking of Franny's chair. And then there were three sounds from the direction of the door—all the same, and all subdued, yet quite distinct.

I could not move. I wanted to scream and couldn't get my breath. And then the rocker slowed to a stop, and there was a dull thud.

CHAPTER SEVENTEEN

I KNEW that Franny had fallen to the floor, that she was dead and that someone had murdered her without even coming into the room.

I found my voice suddenly and loosed scream after shrill scream, until the door was pushed wide and someone snapped on the light. Jennie and Mr. Keith stood staring at me, their faces pallid, and Oliver was directly behind them, peering over their shoulders.

I pointed to Franny's huddled body and then turned my head away. Mr. Keith bent over her and asked Oliver to give him a lift, but Oliver said no in a scared voice and added that it was a matter for the police. Mr. Keith agreed at once and stepped back.

"Is she dead then?" I asked unsteadily. "Are you sure?"

"She's dead all right, poor soul," Jennie whispered.

Allan came in, followed closely by Ross. Ross went rather white when he saw her and lit a cigarette with hands that were visibly shaking.

Allan looked at Franny, and then at me and asked curtly, "What happened?"

I had to fight for my voice again, and he turned and rapped out an order to Mr. Keith about phoning for Detective Hatton, after which he returned his attention to me and said briefly, "Go on."

"How do you know she's dead?" I said hysterically. "Why don't you send for the doctor?"

"Merciful God, girl!" Jennie cried. "Look at her!"

I looked then and turned my head sharply away again in horror. The face was one mass of blood, and there seemed to be two holes in the head and one in the neck. She had been shot then—three times, to make certain of it—and the silencer used on the gun. I thought dully that whoever had done it must have had good aim to have found his mark every time from the doorway, and with Franny rocking constantly.

Allan was saying, "Pull yourself together, can't you? And tell me what happened."

I told them the whole thing, and to my horror I saw disbelief on every face.

Allan said, "Are you trying to tell me that someone came here and shot her, while you were in the room, and that you saw nothing?"

"Why don't you listen?" I cried desperately. "I've told you the rocking chair is in full view from the door, and my bed is behind the door. The door had been pushed farther open—I saw that—and whoever did it shot from there."

Allan shrugged. "We'll wait for the police and see what they have to say."

We waited for about fifteen minutes that seemed like as many hours, with poor Franny lying on the floor, and then Mr. Keith returned with Detective Hatton and Bill. Detective Hatton seemed thoroughly upset, and he questioned me courteously but with great attention to detail for some time. The others had only one story to tell in common—they had all been sleeping in their beds and had been awakened by my screams.

He presently sent us out of the room, and I put on my robe and went down to the kitchen with Jennie. Mr. Keith stationed himself in the front hall to admit the doctor, and Oliver, after prowling restlessly for a while, at last joined Jennie and me in the kitchen.

"For God's sake, Jen," he said, "make some coffee."

"I'm making tea; I have the kettle on. I know Mr. Keith will want his tea after all this."

"Oh, for Chrissake," said Oliver, "I can't drink that lunatic soup. Can't you make coffee too?"

Jennie set her lips and banged the percolator onto the stove. "It's just imagination and habit, this coffee drinking."

I was sent off to ask Hattie—provided she was up—and Allan and Ross if they would have coffee, as long as Jennie was making it, although I was to delete this last.

They were not downstairs, so I went up to the second floor. Hattie must have been peeking out of her door, for it opened as soon as I appeared, and she hailed me. Her face was very white, and she was trembling. She said, "How dreadful!" several times and made me repeat my story from start to finish. She seemed to believe me, too, and I felt almost grateful. She nodded once or twice and then began to shiver, and I could hear her teeth chattering. In the end she burst into tears and sobbed out that she could not stand it.

I tried to soothe her and got her back into bed. She refused the coffee, but said she thought that a cocktail might help her. I told her I'd get Mr. Keith to make one and bring it to her.

She said, "No—no, have Oliver bring it up. I must speak to him, anyway."

I left her at that and made my way along the hall to Allan's room, where I knocked. He flung the door open and looked at me coldly and in silence. "Jennie sent me to ask if you want coffee," I said, edging away.

He stood aside and said, "Come in," without much expression.

I went in and remained uneasily just inside the door. Ross was sitting in the armchair with his head and shoulders drooping. He said to me absentmindedly, "Hello, toots," but he did not really look at me.

Allan said, "There's a lot that I still don't understand about this. In the first place, what was my sister doing in your room?"

I told him patiently, but he did not seem satisfied. "Why didn't you tell me about it?"

"But I did!" I protested. "I was always trying to tell you about her—only you wouldn't listen."

He blamed me, of course, for not making the situation clearer. He said it seemed rather terrible that we could not have saved her, since she had actually told me what was going to happen. In fact, I received a thorough dressing down. I gave up trying to explain after a while and just stood there, staring at the carpet.

Ross broke it up at last. He said, "Lord, Allan, let the kid alone. You know very well that Fran was cracked, and if she'd told you what she told Ellen you'd have advised her to go to bed and sleep it off."

Allan turned away rather abruptly and dropped down onto the bed. "Yes," he said heavily. "I suppose that's right."

I started to retreat, but Allan raised his eyes and said, "Wait a minute, there's another matter." He looked at Ross. "This concerns you. It seems you've made a thorough search of my room and Franny's. Is that right?"

"Quite right," said Ross easily.

"Why?"

"Well, as a matter of fact, I've been robbed."

"Are you implying that I'm the robber?"

Ross shifted his position and said, "Never mind the sarcasm; the thing's easily explained. You know what difficulty I have in trying to keep myself in funds. Some time ago I decided to leave a roll in this house, as a sort of reserve; it wasn't a bad idea, because I could not spend it impulsively, since I had to come all the way out here to get it. It's been a lifesaver on several occasions, and I always replenished it when I was in clover. Just recently, however, the entire nest egg disappeared."

"It sounds completely screwy to me," Allan observed.

"It would. But if you were the observant type you'd know that there are two kinds of people in this world—those who live above their means, and those—"

"All right," said Allan impatiently, "get on with it. Why did you expect to find the money in Franny's room or mine?"

"I didn't. Those were merely the end of a long trail. I was determined to search the place from attic to cellar before I spoke to you about it."

"Did you find it?"

"No," said Ross, "and my financial embarrassment is acute."

I had been too interested through this explanation to try and get away, but now Allan noticed me and said rudely, "Get out."

I was suddenly furious. He had made me stay when I wanted to go, and yet his attitude suggested that I had been eavesdropping.

"I won't get out," I said angrily, "until you answer me about the coffee."

He turned on me and barked, "What did you say to me?"

I spoke my piece again, a trifle louder.

Ross laughed heartily, but Allan started toward me, and my old fear got the better of me. I ran. Halfway down the hall I stopped and nearly went back, but not quite. I went down the back stairs and returned to the, kitchen.

"You're a bright one," Jennie said. "You've only been gone about an hour—that's all."

"Mrs. Hattie wants a cocktail," I said, "and Messrs. Allan and Ross would not say."

Jennie said, "Well, that's just dandy. Now we know just what to do."

"If I were you I'd simply wait a bit and serve them all an early breakfast," I suggested.

She adopted this plan in the end, but only after she had reformed it enough to sound as though it were her own idea. We served breakfast at twenty past six and had our own at seven.

It was not a cheerful meal. Mr. Keith attempted to do some deducing, but could not get beyond the conclusion that the gun with the silencer had been used to kill Franny. I agreed and tried to describe the sounds that I had heard.

Oliver interrupted with an irrelevant remark about his appendix: It had been bothering him for years, he said, and he thought he'd have it out; it had to be done sometime, anyway.

Jennie approved this as a good idea and added that it would be a nice rest from all the horror, and she wished she had an organ that needed looking to.

Oliver put in, as an afterthought, that the operation would have to be paid for, and he was embarrassed, and how about Mr. Keith lending him a little something.

Mr. Keith said no.

I was put to work after breakfast. I was mopping up the front hall some time later, when the doorbell rang.

I opened the door, since I was right beside it, and confronted a short, stout individual who was wearing his stiff collar back to front. He said, "I wish to see Miss Frances Barton. She is expecting me this morning."

My eyes popped, and I think my mouth fell open a bit.

"Come, come, my good girl," he said impatiently; "tell Miss Barton that Mr. Evans is here. She said it was urgent."

CHAPTER EIGHTEEN

I RETREATED a step and found Detective Hatton at my elbow. He said, "Come in, Mr. Evans. I'd like to have a word with you."

"But I have no time," the Rev. Evans protested fussily. "The funeral, you know, this morning. And Miss Barton insisted that I see her first." He turned to me and added, "Kindly inform Miss Barton at once that I am here."

"Run along, Ellen," Detective Hatton said, giving me a warning glance. He ushered Mr. Evans into the drawing room, and as I made my way to the back hall I saw the folding doors close upon them. I kept right on walking in a small circle and returned to the front hall, where I glued an ear to the drawing-room doors in Mr. Keith's best style.

Detective Hatton was saying, "It's very important, Mr. Evans, for you to tell me what Miss Barton wanted to see you about."

"You must understand, sir," said Mr. Evans with mild obstinacy, "that I cannot break Miss Barton's confidence without her consent."

"I'm afraid we'll have to skip Miss Barton's consent. She was murdered last night."

Mr. Evans was suitably shocked and vastly indignant at the killing of a harmless maiden lady. I mentally agreed with him. I had become almost fond of Franny, and it seemed pretty beastly for anyone to kill her in cold blood.

"She must have known something," Mr. Evans was saying. "She must positively have known something, and that is why she wanted to see me."

"Didn't she give any explanation when she asked you to come?"

"She called me on the telephone and said that she had decided to tell me everything and leave it to me to do as I thought best. She wanted me to come last night, but unfortunately I had an engagement."

Detective Hatton loosed a fancy groan. "Good God, man! Why didn't you go? Or at least tell us she intended to confide in you? The thing would probably have been cleared up by now, and perhaps the woman's life saved."

It sounded as though Mr. Evans had stood up, and when he spoke his voice was loaded with pompous dignity. "My conscience is quite clear, sir. I had a sick call last night—one that I could not possibly have disregarded. And if you want to know what I really think, my good man, it is that the fault lies with you. It was announced at the inquest that Miss Barton knew something, and apparently you made no attempt to find out what it was. Further, you don't appear to have had her guarded or protected in any way, although you should have feared the very thing that has happened."

I decided to leave at that point, to avoid being discovered by the outraged minister on his way to the door, but as I straightened my stiff back I was yanked away. It was Mr. Keith, and I could see that he was very angry. "Don't you ever, Ellen McTavish, do a thing like that again," he said, enunciating clearly and emphasizing each word. He steered me down the hall to the kitchen, where Jennie, emerging from the pantry, raised her sandy eyebrows in surprise. "Heavenly days! What's she been doing now?" she asked.

"Eavesdropping," said Mr. Keith sternly. He released me and settled his cuffs. "Now, miss, you're to tell me every word you heard."

Jennie's small eyes became eager, and she moved closer to us. "Mind, you're not to leave any of it out."

I swallowed a desire to laugh and told them the whole thing. Jennie lost interest early on and disappeared into the pantry again, but Mr. Keith seated himself and, placing the tips of his fingers together, began to deduce.

"You see, Miss Franny knew something—that's quite evident—and she would not tell. Now the question is, why wouldn't she tell?"

I said, "She was afraid—or else she was fond of the person who she'd be telling on."

Mr. Keith spared me a look of scorn, and Jennie, closing the pantry door firmly behind her, said, "Shut up, you."

Mr. Keith fell to ruminating once more. "The gun was not found—has not been found yet—and that means that the murderer probably has it still. Keeps it somewhere, ready and waiting for another victim, perhaps. I have searched, and the detectives have searched, and yet it must be somewhere. And this time it must be found."

Jennie gave a gasping little cry, and I muttered, "You're damned right."

"If somebody doesn't find it I'm going to leave," Jennie declared in a panic.

Mr. Keith washed her with a glance of chilly scorn. "The Keiths are not rats to leave a sinking ship."

"I'm no Keith—only by marriage," Jennie quavered.

"As long as you bear my name," he said loftily, "you will conduct yourself as a Keith should."

"The Kirks weren't so bad," Jennie muttered, apparently referring to her own family, but the words were too low for Mr. Keith's ear.

"Isn't it time for lunch?" I asked, yawning.

"Hear the girl!" Jennie shrilled. "And it's not ten o'clock yet."

I was put back to work and had to suppress an almost unbearable longing to get away from the gloomy house and everyone in it. Work was better than sitting and thinking, though, and I went off to tackle the study.

Detective Hatton presently joined me, and I was startled to see that he had the little memorandum book I had found in Allan's desk. I had forgotten it completely and, as far as I could remember, had left it lying around somewhere in my room.

He showed it to me. "Is this yours?"

"No," I said nervously. "Not mine. I—found it."

"Where?"

"Oh, somewhere," I said confusedly. "Down here. In the—in the front hall." I was conscious of a fleeting thought that I had never done so much lying in my life before.

"Do you know who owns it?"

"No," I said guiltily and hoped that Allan's name was not scrawled somewhere in the thing to link him up with that incriminating bit about seeing George by the fourteenth.

The detective made me show him the exact spot in the hall where I had found the wretched book, and after I had chosen a place by the front door he stooped down to get a closer view.

"I've cleaned out here since I found it," I said hastily.

"No doubt. Now why did you take it up to your room instead of making some effort to locate the owner? If you were in a hurry you could have put it in the sitting room where it would almost certainly be returned to the right person."

"Oh well—I was in a hurry, and I simply put the thing in my pocket and never thought of it again until I went to my room. I took it out of my pocket then and promptly forgot all about it."

"What pocket?" he asked coldly and plunged me into confusion. I had been wearing my robe, of course, when I found the book in Allan's desk, but my uniform had no pocket of any description.

I blinked at Detective Hatton, suddenly remembered the apron that Jennie had tied around me and which had a huge pocket and breathed again. I explained about the apron and felt like the winner of a quiz contest.

He left me rather abruptly, and I took an idle look at myself in the hall mirror. I was shocked. Never, in my memory, had I looked so utterly crummy. My uniform and apron were unironed, of course, and seemed dirtier than before I had washed them. My hair looked like a bird's nest, and my face was completely bare of makeup. I made up my mind firmly and on the instant and went straight to the kitchen.

"Jennie," I said, "my uniform needs ironing."

"You're telling me," said Jennie briefly.

"And I don't know how to iron."

She laughed. "Before you waste good breath saying it—nothing doing. Maybe Oliver will do it for you—or Bill."

I said, "Oh no, neither Oliver nor Bill. You're going to do it, because I'll pay you five dollars if it's done within the next hour."

She dropped a potato and a small paring knife into the sink and turned around to goggle at me. "Are you daft?"

"No," I said, "and you'd better make up your mind. Either you want that five or you don't. Terms strictly in advance, of course."

She did my ironing, complaining, but in a milder vein, and several times she looked at me in a puzzled fashion. The ironing equipment was in the basement, so I took off my dress, and she made me put on one of her fearful aprons, which covered everything but my arms and shoulders. She directed me to go straight up to my room then and get the five.

When I got to the third floor, I found Bill lounging in the hall and all my belongings piled on the floor. The door to my room was closed as far as it would go.

Bill said, "Hello, babe," and I said, "Hello,' " and looked at my things and then at the closed door.

"We're movin' you out, kid," he explained. "You're takin' the next room. Here, I'll help you with your things."

My new room was smaller, and I would have preferred to be the length of the corridor away, but at least it had no rocking chair, for which I was vastly thankful.

"Is she still in there?" I whispered, indicating my old room.

Bill nodded. "Gee, babe," he said admiringly, "you sure got a lot of ideas about dressin' snappy on the job."

I glanced down at my apron. "You like this?" I asked, surprised.

"Yeah," said old Bill. "I like the top part."

I looked in the mirror at the top part and saw what he meant. It was like an evening dress with low *décolletage* and strap shoulders. "It's a little warm around the knees when I'm working hard," I said critically. "I'm designing one now that's just like this, except the bottom part is shorts."

There was a step on the stair just then, and Bill rushed out to his post in case it turned out to be Detective Hatton.

I cleaned myself up thoroughly and ended by brushing and combing my hair vigorously and carefully making up my face. I slipped five dollars into my pocket and decided that I looked vastly better, although I felt terrible. My head was aching furiously, and I took some aspirin, which reminded me of Franny and sent me hurrying down the stairs.

Halfway down the last flight I realized that I was using the front stairs. I stopped and wondered whether to go back and start over again or continue down and hope that the Keiths would not hear of it.

As I hesitated I noticed that the dust was thick on the wood each side of the plum-colored carpet on every step. I sighed, wondering when Jennie would catch up with me about it, and then I saw a smudge in the dust and bent closer to examine it.

It was the print of an animal's paw again.

CHAPTER NINETEEN

So THERE WAS some kind of an animal in the house—there must be. Some queer, ghostly creature that left its mark in the dust and yet was never seen. I shuddered and, clutching at the banister, made my way slowly down the stairs. At the foot I came face to face with Allan, and his expression told me that my neck was out again. I supposed I was at fault in using the front stairs, so I said primly, "I'm sorry about not using the back way, Mr. Allan, but Jennie sent me to see if the front stairs needed cleaning."

He glanced at the stairs, and I knew by his slightly altered expression that my presence on them was not the current transgression.

"I understand that the stairs are supposed to be cleaned once a day, whether they need it or not," he said distantly, "and you'll remember to do them hereafter." He gave me a brief, comprehensive running over with his eyes and came to the matter in hand. "I absolutely forbid you to appear again in this house wearing a costume of that sort. You should be able to make the men without going to those lengths."

He was always able to make me furious, but I tried to hold myself in and said carelessly, "I'm sorry you don't like it, sir. I thought it looked rather attractive; I know Bill was intrigued. But tastes differ. I have a dear old aunt who feels the way you do. She always wears long black stockings with her bathing suit, and—"

"That will do," said Allan coldly. "And I warn you again to keep yourself as much in the background as possible for your own sake."

He walked off, and I longed to throw one of the knickknacks, of which the hall was overfull, at his retreating back. I felt that it would be refreshing, if dangerous, to break down his dignity for once.

Jennie had my uniform and apron finished when I got back to the kitchen, so I changed into them then and there and hoped that Mr. Keith would not walk in on me and get himself all embarrassed.

I felt trim and clean and fresh once more. Jennie ordered me off at once to several bits of dirty housework, and I looked at her in dismay. "Oh, Jennie, I can't. I'll get all grubby again."

"Well! I never did in all my born days!" she said, astounded. I could see that once she got her breath she was going on to harsher things and I knew that my clean outfit would not soften her heart, so I quickly introduced a diversion.

"Do you know that there is a ghost animal in this house?" I asked, glancing over my shoulder.

She was holding a spoon in her hand, and it dropped and bounced from the table to the floor with a loud clatter.

"What—what do you mean?" she gasped.

"What I say."

"But, how do you—what have you seen?"

"I haven't seen it; nobody has. But it's here," I declared, dropping my voice to a whisper.

She stared at me, speechless with fear, and at that moment Mr. Keith walked into the kitchen.

"They have all gone to the funeral," he observed, "and we are to have lunch at two o'clock precisely."

Jennie turned to him and quavered, "As if I wasn't scared to death already—this girl says there's a—a ghost animal in the house."

"My good woman," said Mr. Keith reprovingly, "how many times must I tell you that there are no such things as ghosts?" He turned to me and added sternly, "Explain yourself, Ellen."

I told him about the two paw marks, but he was unimpressed. "There are no animals in this house; I should certainly know about it if there were. The marks you saw were something else. Something coincidental."

"Coincidental?" I asked politely.

"Coincidental," said Mr. Keith, rolling the word comfortably off his tongue.

Jennie appeared to be so relieved that I was afraid her mind would return to housework, so I said, "All right—coincidental, if you say so. But what supernatural agency was rocking the chair in my room? Because I saw it rocking all by itself."

Jennie hysterically called me a liar first, and then she sat down at the table and burst into tears.

"What are we going to do?" she sobbed. "I can't stand it—that's all."

I was surprised to see that Mr. Keith looked shaken himself. He touched a tongue to his dry lips, rallied and said bravely, "Don't be silly. You know quite well that chairs cannot rock by themselves."

I said, "This one did."

"It was Alice's rocking chair," Jennie whispered, "that one in her room. Alice loved it and often sat rocking in it. Don't you remember? Miss Franny said she loved it so that she wouldn't have it taken out of her room when she got the new bedroom suite. And now she's coming back to it and rocking in it, the way she always liked to."

"Hold your tongue!" said Mr. Keith sharply. "The thing must be explainable in some perfectly ordinary way."

"Go ahead," I said, "you explain it."

He said, "Certainly. When I think it over I shall do so."

The telephone rang, and Mr. Keith handed it over to me with a brief word to the effect that it was Jane Schmaltz again.

I took over, and from the corner of my eye I saw Mr. Keith slide quickly out of the kitchen, and knew that he was going to listen in somewhere.

"Listen, Jane," I said clearly, "I haven't got them and I won't be able to."

"My dear, I know," said Selma excitedly. "Isn't it awful? I only just heard about it—read it, I mean. I happened to pick up a newspaper."

"All right," I said, with my mind on Mr. Keith. "See you sometime."

"Hey, listen!" she squealed. "Can't I help you, or something?"

"No. Get off the phone. I'll get in touch with you later."

She got off, and I drew a long breath.

Oliver came in and said, "Listen—what about some grub?"

"I thought you were driving Madam Hattie to the funeral?" Jennie said in some surprise.

"Madam Hattie thought so too." Oliver grinned. "But Allan comes along and puts a couple feet in the gravy and tells her she's got to go with him and Ross. She was plenty burned about it too."

"Mr. Keith says you should call them Mr. Allan and Mr. Ross, even when they can't hear you," Jennie observed.

"Catch me wasting my breath like that," Oliver said amiably.

Mr. Keith returned to the kitchen, and we presently sat down to lunch.

"I wish I could have gone to the funeral," said Jennie through a mouthful of potato.

"Why didn't you mention it?" asked Mr. Keith. "I am sure it could have been arranged."

"Well, but who was to get the lunch?"

Mr. Keith waved his hand at me, and while I laughed dryly Jennie curled her lip in scorn.

I wanted a cigarette after my lunch, and since I had none with me and could not smoke in the kitchen without a fight, anyway, I decided to slip up to my room. On the second flight of stairs I met Bill making his way down. He was mopping at his forehead, and when he saw me he bunched the handkerchief back into his pocket and grinned sheepishly. "Gives me the creeps up there. And I wish the hell it would stop raining."

I sighed. "So do I."

"I'm gonna feed my face," Bill said, shaking himself. "Maybe what's the matter with me, I need food."

"Maybe," I said and went on up to the third floor. I didn't like it there any better than Bill did, and I decided to get the cigarettes and have my smoke in a more cheerful spot.

The hall was dim, and I looked around rather fearfully and saw the door to the room where Franny was still lying open a crack. Beyond that there was another small room; and across the hall, two large rooms, occupied by Oliver and the Keiths, with the bathroom between them. Impulse suddenly decided me to do a little snooping, and without thinking twice I stepped across and entered the Keiths' bedroom.

As I had expected, it was immaculately clean. There were picture postcards stuck into every inch of available space in the mirror, and I shamelessly inspected them. They seemed mostly to be from friends; several of them were from Scotland, and I found one from Mr. Evans. He had sent it from Atlantic City, and it informed the Keiths, who might not have known otherwise, that the weather was beautiful.

There was nothing else of interest, and I went on to Oliver's room. It was messy, untidy and dusty, with overflowing ashtrays and match stubs lying around on the floor. I wrinkled my nose in disgust and backed out again.

I went to my own room and got the cigarettes, and as I started out I heard someone coming up the stairs. I retreated and half closed the door, and I saw Mr. Keith walk across to his room. He came out again almost immediately and went into the bathroom, and to my surprise I heard him drawing water in the bathtub. I remembered Jennie making a ceremony of his weekly bath only yesterday, and I stood there with my forehead tied into a puzzled frown.

But he did not take a bath. He came out as soon as he had shut off the water and went straight downstairs.

I walked over to the bathroom and looked at the tub. It was filled with water, and when I stuck a tentative finger into it I found that the water was cold.

A cold bath just left there. Was he as crazy as poor Franny had been? Or was there some reason behind it?

I went slowly back to my room and lit a cigarette. I had forgotten about finding a more cheerful spot, and I sat down, listening to the rain and thinking about Mr. Keith.

It was some minutes before I realized that I was listening to something besides the rain.

The chair in the next room was rocking.

CHAPTER TWENTY

I SPRANG UP, with the sweat starting out on my forehead, but nothing would have induced me to go into that room and investigate. I fled to the kitchen in search of Bill.

Mr. Keith and Oliver had gone, and Jennie was preparing lunch for the family. Bill sat at the table behind an overflowing plate and raised his head to me as I came in, with both cheeks bulging.

"It's someone—something—in that room where Franny is," I said breathlessly. "I heard the chair rocking."

Jennie turned from the sink with a little moan and was so upset that she forgot to scold me for having run away after lunch instead of helping.

Bill deflated his face by swallowing twice and stood up with a sigh for his interrupted meal. He started up the stairs, and Jennie and I followed in frightened fascination.

There was no one in the room but Franny when we got there, and the rocking chair was quite still. Bill made a perfunctory search of the entire floor without finding anything, and both he and Jennie passed over the full bathtub without comment. They appeared not to notice it.

Bill invited us to accompany him on a searching expedition to the fourth floor—probably because he was afraid to go alone—and we trailed after him like a couple of scared children. Jennie was breathless with excitement and had her eye peeled for ghosts.

There were four rooms up there—two on each side of the hall, and no bathroom. We made a methodical search, but when we came to Alice's room Jennie remained determinedly in the hall. "It's her bedroom soot in there," she whispered. "She was so fond of it—always said she wouldn't part with it, no matter what."

Bill took a quick look around the room, and so did I. I was immediately struck by a nagging sense of something different, but I could not place it, and I had to follow Bill when he went out because I was afraid to stay there by myself.

We returned to the third floor, and Bill asked me if I would mind mounting guard in the hall while he finished his lunch. I did mind, but I reluctantly agreed to do it. I asked Jennie to stay with me, but she refused. The family would be home at two, she said, and lunch must be ready for them.

They went off and left me there, and I lit a cigarette and wandered aimlessly around the hall. I kept pretty close to the head of the stairs for the most part, so that I could make a quick getaway in case it was needed.

Nothing happened though. There was no sound from any of the rooms, and the rocking chair seemed to be taking a rest.

Mr. Keith came up the stairs after a while and gave me a look of reproof. "Why are you wasting your time here, Ellen? There is plenty to be done in the kitchen."

I explained, with a certain amount of gusto, and reproof changed to perplexity on his face. He ran a troubled hand through his hair and muttered, "How is it possible? The chair *cannot* rock of itself."

He suddenly made straight for the room where Franny lay, and I followed timidly to the door. But he merely made a brief search and then came out.

In the hall he paused and went into a brown study, and then he raised his head and walked into the bathroom. He left the door open, and without any attempt at concealment, stooped over and opened the drain in the bathtub. Curiosity burned in me to such a degree that when he came out into the hall again I simply stepped up and asked him why he had filled the tub with water, in the first place, and why he had subsequently let it run out without using it.

He elevated his brows in faint surprise and said, "You should learn not to ask questions, Ellen. It's an unfortunate habit in a young girl," and went on downstairs.

I was so restless and nervous by the time Bill came up that I was almost glad to return to the kitchen and help Jennie.

I set the table, as usual, and since Jennie seemed to regard the meal as an occasion, I was delegated to dining-room service under Mr. Keith.

Hattie appeared to have been weeping buckets, as usual, but she ate like a horse. Allan and Ross were quiet.

They had almost finished the meal, when Hattie announced rather sulkily that she could not stay under the roof for another night.

"Why not?" Allan asked.

"It wouldn't be right," Hattie explained virtuously. "Me alone, and two unmarried men in the house."

"I'm not unmarried yet," Allan said, looking bored.

"Well, of course—I know. But you will be soon, and I have my reputation to think of."

"Ellen or Jennie would be glad to see to your reputation, I'm sure," Allan suggested courteously. "Would you care to have one of them sleep in your room?"

Hattie reddened and said, "No—certainly not. But I don't see why you can't give me some money so that I can go to New York."

Allan said, "I'm sorry, but you couldn't very well go even if I gave you the money. Hatton told me particularly that he expected us all to stay here until this thing has been cleared up."

Hattie burst into tears and sobbed, "Yes—and we'll be killed off one by one while he sits and thinks about it. It isn't fair. It's cruel, and he has no right—"

"Don't be morbid," Allan said, looking bored again. "Just be careful and lock your door at night."

Franny was taken away after lunch, and I found myself crying over her. She had known she was going to be killed and had even told me, and I felt that I should have done something—prevented it in some way.

At about four o'clock a lawyer came out to read George's will. I wondered what there could possibly be to read, since George had presumably been living on Allan. Nevertheless, they all filed into the sitting room, and even the Keiths were summoned to attend. Oliver was sent to the village on a marketing errand, and I hung around in the hall, ostensibly dusting knickknacks.

As Allan went in I heard him say to Ross, "Don't worry, this isn't my idea. Hattie arranged it—everything in order. Elaborate funeral first, and then the bums' rush for home to see what he left you."

After they had all gone in and closed the door I laid my ear to the crack, since Mr. Keith wasn't there to do it for me.

The whole thing seemed pretty silly to me, but it developed that it had been George's wish. As I had supposed, there was no money involved, but George remembered them all with various personal trinkets until he came to Hattie. He left Hattie his love.

Hattie let out a yell at that point: "Wait a minute—what is this? He owned the house, didn't he?"

"No," Allan said quietly. "I bought it from him some years ago."

"What do you mean, 'bought it from him'?" Hattie shrieked. "I know he owned it—he told me so. He said you were paying him rent."

"I was giving him something to live on," Allan cut in decisively, "and I'll give you an allowance if you'll shut up. But you'll get nothing whatever if you make any further vulgar disturbance, and you can be very sure that I mean what I say."

Hattie began to cry hysterically, and she rushed out of the room in such hurry that she nearly knocked me down, but she did not seem to notice me. I fled to the kitchen before I could be discovered by anyone else.

Oliver had returned, and he asked me to take a parcel up to Hattie. "You know how it is, babe. If I take it up I'll get stuck, and I don't want that gumshoe catchin' on."

He winked at me, and I shrugged and took the parcel.

I found Hattie lying on her bed. She had stopped crying and looked mad enough to chew nails. I gave her the package and explained that Oliver had sent it up.

Her face reddened, and she asked angrily, "Why didn't he bring it up himself?"

"I don't know, madam," I said innocently. "I believe he was busy."

She regarded me speculatively for a moment and then abruptly ordered me to sit down. I sat and wished that I could smoke.

"Are you in love with Oliver?" she asked flatly.

I said, "No, madam."

"I don't believe you. I've seen you rolling your eyes at him."

"Oh no, madam," I said, registering astonishment. "I have never—"

"I tell you I've seen you," she interrupted angrily. "And I'm warning you to lay off or I'll have you fired."

"But I assure you, madam—"

"Shut up," said Hattie, "and get out."

I got out and decided resentfully that I was constantly being told to shut up and get out. I folded my lips into a thin line and made a mental resolution to say nothing more to anybody, and then it came to me that I probably looked like Jennie, with my mouth that way, so I relaxed.

Jennie and Mr. Keith were discussing their bequests in the kitchen. Mr. Keith was disappointed, because he had fully expected to receive George's electric shaver—George having made some such indication in an expansive moment—and had been left George's electric clock instead. The clock was not particularly appreciated, since Mr. Keith already had one.

Jennie was to receive George's small Bible, but she seemed more interested in the disposal of George's big Bible, which had been left to Franny.

"He hadn't used it for years, that big Bible," Jennie said thoughtfully. "It's up on the fourth floor in that room where Alice's furniture is—on the bureau."

Something clicked in my brain, and I suddenly knew what had been different about Alice's room. The Bible was no longer there.

"Are you sure it's still there—on the bureau?" I asked cautiously.

"It's always been there," Jennie said positively. "Nobody would dream of moving it. I know Mr. George used to say that if anyone tried to make off with that Bible they wouldn't get farther than the next floor down before God would strike them dead. You see, he left it in that room for Alice."

CHAPTER TWENTY-ONE

I SAT DOWN and said, "What are you talking about, Jennie? Do you mean to tell me that George was loopy too?"

Jennie gaped at me, but Mr. Keith frowned. "You are impertinently forward, Ellen. A person is not necessarily unbalanced because he believes in a spirit world."

I said, "No—but by the time a spirit reaches the spirit world, I shouldn't think it would need to read the Bible any more."

But you couldn't corner Mr. Keith. "Quite," he said smoothly. "Nevertheless, you overlook the fact that Mr. George did not expect his dead sister to read the Bible. He merely wanted her to know that he had given it to her."

I stared at him and he stared back without a trace of confusion.

"Do you mean," I said at last, "that he gave her the Bible after she was dead?"

"Exactly. She had always admired it, and after she died and they put her things up on the fourth floor Mr. George had the Bible put there, too, because she had liked it."

I nodded thoughtfully and felt obliged to admit that George might have been foolishly sentimental, but not necessarily cracked.

Mr. Keith went on, "He left the Bible to Miss Franny, because he knew she would see that it was kept up in that room where he wanted it. Now that Miss Franny has passed on, Jennie is naturally anxious to know that whoever gets the book will carry on the tradition."

Jennie nodded gravely. "You see, if anyone brings it down they might get as far as our floor and then be struck dead."

"No kidding," I said scornfully, and Mr. Keith cleared his throat in a manner to warn me that making fun of his wife was not permissible.

I eased out then, because I wanted to verify my conviction that the Bible had disappeared. I was sure that I had noticed a large, black book when I first looked the room over, and just as sure that it was gone when Bill and I investigated.

I found that Bill had gone when I reached the third floor, and I felt very much alone. My anxiety to get to Alice's room waned sharply, and I stood at the foot of the stairs, hesitating. I glanced nervously at the room from which they had taken Franny and saw that the door was closed as far as it would go. The hall was dim and quiet, and I began to shiver. I knew that I would have to go up the flight in front of me at once, or rush downstairs again in a panic.

I went up. The goose pimples were out on my arm, and my hair prickled as I reached the landing, and I could hear the incessant patter of rain on the roof over my head. I thought despairingly that if we could only see the sun again the whole thing would not be so dreadful.

I stepped quietly across to Alice's room and opened the door and wondered at the same time why I was being so stealthy about it.

There was no book on the bureau, but I found a large, square mark in the dust and knew that my conviction had been right. Suddenly, and quite unbidden, there leaped into my mind a picture of Franny carrying that great Bible down the stairs and being struck down in the rocking chair in my room.

I lost the last shreds of my courage and fled down the stairs in an utter panic. I had got all the way to the front hall before I realized that I had again used the front stairs, and as luck would have it, Allan was just coming out of the drawing room.

I backed up against the wall and wished that I could make myself invisible. I was sure he hated the sight of me, and I had a nervous fear of being hurt by the disagreeable things he always said to me. I supposed that I might have deserved some of them, but I was not quite sure.

He glanced at me and said, "Come into the study. I want to talk to you."

I headed toward the study in silence and feeling something like Marie Antoinette on the way to the guillotine.

He followed me into the room and closed the door. "You may sit down."

I said, "Thank you, sir," and perched myself uneasily on the edge of a chair.

"Wrong role," he said, looking down at me. "Have you forgotten the secret-lovers angle? You ought to throw yourself onto my chest and call me 'darling.' " He swung a chair around to face me and sat down. "That's the worst of all these lies, Calisthenics—they're apt to trip you up."

"You can haul me over the coals," I said desperately, "and throw me to Jennie, but, *please,* don't call me Calisthenics. It puts my teeth on edge."

"Don't change the subject," he said, with his dark eyes on my face. "Now it seems that Selma's divorce went through without a hitch—and without her or her lawyer finding out about our secret passion. Detective Hatton apparently lived up to his promise of secrecy, but it's conditional on his clearing up this thing within a few days. I'm determined that it shall be cleared up within a few days. Poor Franny should have been saved." He paused, frowning, and added, "There doesn't seem to be any sense to it. Who could have killed her—and why?"

"It's obvious, isn't it?"

He looked up at me quickly.

"I mean," I said earnestly, "that she certainly knew why George was sitting up in the dining room every night, and I think it's just as certain that she knew who killed him."

"But Franny could hardly have been as stupid as that," he said. "If she had actually known anything she would not just have sat there and waited."

"Well, but she didn't really know," I said slowly. "She was guessing, and her guess must have been right. She intended confiding in Mr. Evans and asking his advice, but he was not able to see her that night. I'm sure that she felt the danger was close to her then—perhaps she was afraid that someone had listened in when she was telephoning Mr. Evans."

Allan frowned and shook his head. "She should have come to me. But Franny and George took all their problems to Mr. Evans—wouldn't listen to anyone else."

"She must have known something about the fourteenth," I suggested. "She fainted when she saw the mark on the calendar."

He said sharply, "What do you mean? When?"

I explained and added, "You never asked me what had upset her; you merely said that she often had fainting spells."

He nodded grimly. "She did. But she must have known that George was sitting in the dining room night after night, and when she saw that date encircled she knew that whatever was blowing up had come to a head, so she fainted."

I nodded slowly, and he said, "Now, to get back. Hatton is a bit sentimentally inclined, and when I told him I was having difficulty in avoiding you he more or less asked me to treat you kindly."

I squirmed in my seat and gazed at him mutely.

"Bill is going to be on guard in the front hall tonight," he went on. "He's gone home now to catch some sleep. Hatton told him that if he saw you creeping down to meet me in the study he was to look the other way and forget about it. Therefore, you are to creep down to meet me here at about twelve-thirty tonight—and make sure that Bill sees you. I have told the last lie I intend to about your presence in this house, so that if the secret-passion story falls through I shall give Hatton the truth. So you'd better act your part well—or you'll be in trouble."

"Twelve-thirty," I said feebly. "Must creep down here—full view of Bill."

He nodded, said, "Right," and opened the door.

I went to the kitchen on air. I didn't suppose it meant anything, but I couldn't help being proud because I had a date with Mr. Allan.

Jennie gave me the usual abuse, which had to do with my absence when there was work to be done, and she put me on the table-setting assignment.

"Time for the evening meal already?" I asked, surprised.

"It's after five," Jennie snapped.

I imitated a dray horse until six o'clock, when I was permitted a few minutes to run upstairs and tidy myself for service at the table.

I forced myself up to the third floor over a multitude of nervous fears and made a rush for my room. I stopped and listened then, but everything was quiet, and there was no sound of the rocking chair.

I made a hasty cleanup and went out into the hall, and then I started to think about Franny and how, if she had brought that Bible down, it ought to be in my old room. I moved over to the door, took a deep breath and plunged in.

The Bible was there. It was in a corner on the floor, but it had been badly chewed and scratched.

CHAPTER TWENTY-TWO

I RETURNED to the kitchen in a hurry, while my thoughts scampered with the frustrated energy of a cageful of squirrels. Franny must have brought that Bible downstairs, and Franny had been struck down on the third floor. But the Bible was in very poor condition, and nobody had mentioned that. Chewed and scratched—chewed! The animal, of course. There was an animal in the house, and it had been at that book. I wondered, shuddering, why they all denied the presence of an animal, denied it so positively. And yet, either they were all wrong, or I was getting to be as loopy as Franny had been.

Jennie greeted me by putting a dish of celery into my hands, and I went on into the dining-room with it. The sliding doors that gave on to the living room were open, and I could see Hattie talking in a low, urgent voice to Allan and Ross. Allan was leaning back in his chair with his eyes half closed, and Ross, sprawled in another chair, drummed nervously on its arm with his fingers and stared blankly at the ceiling. Neither was paying the slightest heed to Hattie, and I felt a bit sorry for her. It must have been a severe blow to her when she found that she was not to get the house as she had supposed. I decided that she had been pretty confident of it when she told Oliver that she meant to have things her way, and perhaps all this low-voiced talk was an effort to have things her way, nevertheless.

I deposited the celery and went back to the kitchen. Jennie gave me a dish of sliced lemon this time and said, "Tell them it's ready."

I took the lemon to the dining room, looked at the three of them in the room beyond and called absentmindedly, "Come and get it."

I was jerked violently back into the serving pantry by Mr. Keith, who snarled furiously. "Don't you ever dare to announce another meal in this house!" He went off himself and made the announcement properly.

During the meal Hattie went on with her monologue when Mr. Keith and I were out of the room, but there was dead silence whenever we came in.

Our own dinner was more cheerful. Mr. Keith was still a bit chilly with me, but I figured that it would wear off eventually. Oliver was in high spirits and wanted to take me to the movies. I refused him several times, but he would not take me seriously. "No dame ever holds out on me when I put the pressure on, babe."

Jennie said, "Maybe you ain't free tonight. Miss Hattie might want to go somewhere."

"She ain't got no dough," Oliver said reasonably. "You can't go much of anywheres with your pockets hangin' inside out."

Jennie clicked her tongue in disapproval, and it wasn't five minutes later that Hattie put her head in the door and peremptorily ordered the car. She said she needed a breath of air.

After she had gone Jennie snickered and said well, anyway, air was cheap, but Oliver scowled ferociously. "I know a road," he muttered, "that'll knock the air out of her."

"You must not show disrespect," Mr. Keith said aloofly.

"I'll show her something one of these days," Oliver declared. "Only I don't know if you'd call it disrespect. Listen, babe," he added, turning to me, "you wait up for me, see? I'll be back early."

"I can't," I said primly. "I want to keep my job."

He started to argue, but Hattie came back to the kitchen with her coat and hat on, and he had to go.

Jennie and I cleared up the kitchen, and we all went upstairs together. My room did not seem as gloomy as usual, for though a chill, misty rain was falling, it was still daylight, and the Keiths could be heard talking cheerfully in their bedroom.

I rested my forehead against the windowpane and stared out, and the daylight seemed to fade all of a sudden while I stood there. My good spirits faded with it, and I drew the shade and turned on the light. I had no book and nothing at all to read, so I decided to take a bath to pass the time. I filled the tub and had just slipped into the warm water when Jennie came banging at the door. She asked me to let her in, because she had some washing to do and she'd never be able to finish it if I didn't let her get started.

I unlocked the door and got back into the tub, and she came in, carrying her laundry. When she saw me she gave a little shriek and averted her face. "I didn't know you were in the tub; why didn't you say so?" she demanded in a shocked voice.

"I didn't know you'd be interested," I said mildly. "But I can stand it if you can."

She went on to the hand basin and started her washing, but she kept her eyes sternly away from me. "I don't believe in all this boldness," she said severely. "I know you girls run around naked and don't care who sees you, but you wouldn't catch me doing it."

"Not even in front of Mr. Keith?" I asked, interested.

The back of her neck became flushed with dark red, and she said haughtily, "Mr. Keith has never seen me in my underbodice—and never will, naturally."

I slipped, from sheer surprise, and my head went completely under the water. When I was breathing normally again I said, "Well—I'm getting out now, so don't peek through the mirror."

Jennie continued to slap her laundry around, while I dried myself, and after a while I said, trying to be casual, "You know that Bible—the big one on Alice's bureau?"

"What about it?" she asked and shivered in the overheated room.

"Is it in good condition?"

"Why, of course," Jennie said, surprised. "Mr. George always kept his things lovely. He was as fussy as a woman. There isn't a mark on that book, or a torn page. That's why I wanted it, only I wouldn't dare take it out of that room, unless I knew he left it to me in his will."

I went back to my room and looked under the bed and into every corner to make sure that the animal was not in with me before I closed the door. It would not close properly either, but I pushed it into the jamb as far as it would go.

I stretched myself comfortably on the bed and then found, to my dismay, that I was dropping off to sleep.

I dared not go to sleep for fear of missing my date at twelve-thirty, so I got up again and moved aimlessly around the room.

I presently heard a step out in the hall and went noiselessly to the door to snoop. To my surprise it was Hattie, and she was quietly making her way up the stairs to the top floor. I let her get out of sight, and then I followed her.

When I reached the upper hall the door to Alice's room was closed, and a thread of light showed beneath it. I could hear Hattie in there, apparently searching, since she seemed to be tearing the place apart.

When I thought I heard her coming out I slipped into the next room—the one in which I had closed the window. I noticed at once that it was open again, and the floor was wet with the rain. I thought ghoulishly that Franny must have opened that window before she died, so that she could lean out and reach up around the roof.

I heard Hattie coming toward me, and I backed into the shadows in the corner of the room. She walked in and stood for a moment, looking at the open window. She went over and started to lower it, and then she stopped and stuck her head out into the rain instead. I saw her stretch her arms up around the roof and then down around the sides of the window. One side held her attention for quite a while, and suddenly she drew her head in and turned swiftly away. She was stuffing something down the front of her dress as she practically ran from the room.

She had left the window open, and after a moment's hesitation I went over and took a look at it. It was a dormer window, with shingles on each side and a slate roof gleaming wetly in the darkness. I felt around the shingles and over the slippery surface of the slate, but there did not seem to be anything in the least out of the ordinary.

And then something brushed against my leg.

I leaped backward and stood for a moment, sweating and shaking and peering into the gloom, but I could see nothing. I turned and fled, and even in my state of panic I retained sense enough to be quiet about it.

But Jennie and Oliver were standing at the bottom of the stairs, looking up.

"What do you think you're doing, girl?" Jennie demanded angrily.

"I went up to look at the Bible," I said faintly. "Only it's gone."

"Gone!" Jennie repeated. "What are you saying? It can't be gone."

She started up the stairs and called an order over her shoulder for me to accompany her. Oliver came along, too, with a hand on my arm, and managed to kiss my cheek on the way up. "Don't do it, chauffeur," I said, pulling away. "It's as much as our jobs are worth."

He said, "Oh, nuts," and attempted to do it again, but I avoided him and went on ahead.

I was still trembling and trying to tell myself that I had imagined that thing brushing against my leg—and knowing all the time that I had not imagined it. I was wearing my robe, and the robe had definitely flattened in against my leg.

Jennie had turned the light on in Alice's room and was standing there, staring. The room was in the wildest disorder. The drawers of the bureau were all open, and Alice's things had been pawed over and thrown about. The bedclothes had been pulled off the bed, and the mattress was half on the floor. Hattie, I reflected, had searched the place to some tune.

Jennie turned on me furiously. "How dare you do a thing like this? Her room—and all her things."

"It was this way when I came up," I explained hastily. "I never touched it."

"That'll be enough of your lies," she cried shrilly. "Nobody has been up here but you."

"Somebody has been up here," I insisted, "because somebody had to make this mess. I didn't."

"I tell you—"

"You'll tell me nothing," I said, losing my temper. "I'm telling you that I did not wreck this room, and I'm not accustomed to being called a liar, and I came up for the sole purpose of looking at that Bible and I found the Bible gone and the room like this."

Jennie backed down, as she always did when anyone stood up to her, and in the little silence that followed we all looked at the bureau.

The Bible was there.

CHAPTER TWENTY-THREE

"Why, what are you talking about?" Jennie said, her voice gone a little hoarse. "The Bible is there."

I went over to have a look at it and discovered that the side which had been chewed and torn was turned to the back, so that it did not show.

Oliver said, "Jeez! Look at this room, willya. Some mess. Looks as if somebody lost their last nickel in here."

"I'm going to get Mr. Keith," Jennie said firmly. "Come on, you two."

We followed her down, and Oliver sidled close to me with a whispered suggestion that I get dressed and go stepping with him, but I managed to shake him off and retired to my own room.

I could hear Jennie talking long and earnestly to Mr. Keith, and after a while they came out of their room and went upstairs. When at last they came down again Jennie went into their bedroom, while Mr. Keith continued on to the second floor. There was a period of silence, and then Allan, Mr. Keith and Bill came tramping up in a group. They went on to the fourth floor, and after having fooled around up there for a while they came down again, marched straight to my door and knocked.

I allowed them to pour in, and Bill addressed me first. "Jennie said you said that there Bible was gone—but it ain't."

"It was not there earlier today," I explained: "The Keiths were talking about it, and I went up to have a look. As a matter of fact, I found it in my old bedroom, and it was all scratched and torn."

Mr. Keith let out an agitated exclamation of some sort, but no one paid any attention to him.

"Then tonight," I went on, "I thought I heard something up there, and I went up. I found that room in complete disorder, but I didn't notice the Bible. It must have been there though, because I went down and found Jennie, and we went straight up again, and there it was."

Bill scratched his head and looked thoroughly confused, while Mr. Keith, still agitated, said, "Excuse me; gentlemen, I must see if the book has been mutilated, as she says."

"You mean then," Allan said slowly, "that someone returned the Bible to its usual place at some time after you saw it in the next room and before you went up there tonight?"

I nodded, and Bill stirred and returned to consciousness. "Wait a minute now—you guys are goin' too fast. Let me get this straight."

We let him get it straight, although it took about twenty minutes, and in the end he merely shrugged and muttered, "So what? I'm only a detective. Nobody learned me to be a minister or a nut doctor. It'll keep until the boss gets here. He'll put two and two together and get five out of it—like always." He loosed a sudden loud guffaw but stopped and looked a trifle self-conscious when he found himself laughing alone.

"Come on," Allan said abruptly. "We'd better go down."

They went off, and I sat on the bed and saw that the alarm clock said eleven-thirty. One more hour to kill somehow and to battle with my growing sleepiness. I had nothing to read and nothing to do but listen to the hateful whispering noises in that gloomy house. I was so tired that only the appointment with Allan kept my eyes from closing up in spite of myself.

The house was quiet, and the only thing that happened during the hour was that Mr. Keith again drew a tubful of water, which apparently he did not use. I saw him, through the crack of my door, as he went quietly into the bathroom, and I saw him leave again when the tub was full and return to his room. I stood at my door and watched for him to come back, but at twenty-five past twelve there was still no sign of him, and I had to go.

I turned out the light in my room and went quietly into the dark hall. A dim light burned in the bathroom, and I could not resist a detour. The tub was still full, and I dipped my fingers in and found that the water was cold. I shook my head and mentally agreed with Bill that the house was badly in need of a resident nut doctor.

The second floor was dark and quiet, and I went on down the front stairs. The lower hall was very brightly lighted, but Bill was nowhere to be seen. I hesitated, remembering that my instructions were to let Bill see me, so that he could report it to Detective Hatton in the morning. I walked around the hall three times, cursing Bill on the way, and then I gave up and went in search of him.

I found him in the kitchen, comfortably wading through a huge meal, and he gave me a cheerful grin. "Hello, baby, where you goin' ?"

I tried to look confused and stammered, "I—er—left something in the study."

"Goin' to the study by way of the kitchen is a long way around," Bill said amiably. "I'll draw you a road map and show you how you can cut mileage." He roared with laughter, and I backed out hastily. He called after me, "That thing you left in the study means you no good, baby. Better pass it up and stay outa trouble."

I hurried through the hall and went on to the study. Allan was stretched comfortably in an armchair, reading a book, and when I came in he glanced up, nodded to me and gestured at a chair. I sat down, folded my hands in my lap and waited.

Allan went on with his reading. Smoke drifted up from a cigarette between his fingers, and a highball stood on a table beside his chair. I watched him for a while with growing resentment, and at last I ventured to ask, "May I have a drink?"

He said, "Certainly," without looking up, and turned a page.

I resisted an impulse to kick the book out of his hands and went over to the liquor cabinet. I began to fumble around with the stuff and promptly broke a glass. Allan raised his head and said impatiently, "For God's sake, what mischief are you getting into now?"

"Sorry," I muttered nervously. "Dropped something."

He returned to his book, and I poured myself a drink. I realized, as soon as I tasted it, that it was much too strong, but I gulped it down, anyway. I felt deflated and annoyed, and I reflected that had I known that my date was going to turn out this way I'd have gone to sleep, regardless of consequences.

I had nothing to do after I finished my drink, so I went back to the cabinet and mixed myself another. I tried to make it weaker, but it was still too strong. I noticed that Allan's glass was empty, and I asked politely if I might replenish it.

He handed it to me without looking up and murmured, "Thank you."

I made a face at the back of his head and made his drink stiffer than my first one. He did not seem to notice it though; he just drank it.

I returned to my chair after several more stiff drinks, and about three minutes later I realized, with rather startling suddenness, that I was very tight. I stood up with a certain amount of difficulty and stumbled to the half-opened window. I was gulping fresh air when I heard a faint noise from the direction of the drawing room. I left the window and made my way to the door and was vaguely annoyed because I made several unnecessary detours quite without my own volition. I listened carefully and could hear Bill making his way through the clutter of trifling furniture in the drawing room; there was no mistaking his asthmatic breathing or the whispered curse he let out when he apparently barked his shin.

I lurched over to Allan, brushed his book onto the floor and fell into his lap. I put my lips against his ear and whispered that Bill was listening at the door.

He nodded and said quietly; "Good. Then we can get this thing over and go to bed."

I said, "Yes sir," but I was hardly prepared for what came next. He caught me roughly against his chest, poured a torrent of breathtaking and expertly endearing words over me and then kissed every available inch of my face and neck.

Once I came up briefly for air and gasped, "Aren't you overdoing it—just a trifle?"

"No," he replied, lowering his voice. "I want to stuff it down their throats once and for all."

I was promptly submerged again, and I noticed that although he presently ran out of words he did not run out of kisses. I was thoroughly annoyed when the door opened, and Bill walked in.

Allan was kissing my left ear and continued to do so, and Bill cleared his throat loudly and managed to inject a certain amount of reproof into the sound.

Allan raised his head then and said angrily, "What the devil are you doing here?" He stood up, which forced me to stand up, too, and I balanced myself only after a couple of dangerous whirls.

"I thought I heard a noise," Bill said, looking embarrassed. "Thought I better investigate."

"It's gratifying to see you taking your job so seriously," Allan said politely. "And now that you have investigated, perhaps you will be good enough to leave us alone."

Bill shuffled, reddened and stood his ground. "I think Ellen ought to go to bed. She has to get up early in the morning."

"Kind of you to be so concerned," Allan said coldly. "I must ask you again to leave us alone."

Bill squared his shoulders, looked Allan in the eye and said bravely, "I'm sorry, sir, but I still think that Ellen would be better off in her own bed upstairs."

I moved in between them and said hastily, "I guess Bill's right. I'll go." I hung my head and started out of the room.

"Good night, my darling," Allan called after me. "I'll see you in the morning." He turned to Bill then, and they closed the door on me. I was left alone in the dark drawing room, surrounded by furniture, with only a shaft of light from the hall to guide me, and in a pretty tolerable state of drunkenness.

I thought it over for a moment and decided simply to walk in as straight a line as possible and let the furniture take care of itself. It worked very well. I found myself in the hall in no time, and although I scattered a few tables and chairs and bruised my legs up a bit, I felt pretty clever.

My head was spinning around in wide, lazy circles by that time, and I got myself up the front stairs only by hanging onto the banister all the way. I had to rest on the second floor, and I began to wonder if I would make my bedroom before I passed out. I plowed on grimly, but I had to stop again, halfway up the next flight, to get my breath. I never made it.

I could see the hall and the dim glow that came from the light in the bathroom—and as I looked I distinctly saw the black paw of an animal.

CHAPTER TWENTY-FOUR

I FLUNG AROUND, with the hair rising all over my head, and practically fell down the half flight of stairs I had so laboriously climbed. I stumbled across the dark hall of the second floor and pushed into a bedroom. The room was dark, and my head was spinning madly, but I somehow groped my way to a bed. I fell flat across it and went out like a light.

Later I struggled up through layers of gray fog to a bright light shining in my eyes and something cold and wet against my face. I tried to turn away and became conscious of an arm across my shoulders, forcing me to sit up. I fought feebly to return to my stupor and was again jerked upward roughly and with no consideration for the fact that my head was attached to my shoulders only by a thin thread. I groaned, and my face was instantly and vigorously washed with a cold, wet towel, blinked, opened my aching eyes and muttered, "Oh, for God's sake, give over."

"Damned little drunkard," Allan's voice said crossly.

"The chronic scold," I said to myself and was surprised to hear my voice come out high and rather foolish. I closed one eye for better focus and cocked the other at the forbidding face hanging over me. "Don't you ever laugh and beat a tambourine?"

"I'll beat something besides a tambourine one of these days," he said ominously and jerked me to my feet. "Come on, damn you, walk."

"Your word," I said politely, "is my law. You want me to walk—but I cannot walk. My feet are so far away."

He began to walk me around the room and demanded, "How the hell did you get in here, anyway?"

I tried to draw myself up in a dignified fashion and nearly overbalanced. He righted me, without gentleness, and I explained, "It was the first room. Any port in a storm."

"Very lucid. What storm, incidentally?"

"What storm?" I repeated. "What lucid storm?" I managed to get both eyes open at the same time and stared at him earnestly. "You wouldn't be sarcastic with me? Not during a lucid storm, when I'm not feeling very well?"

He steered me back to the bed and allowed me to sit down. "I don't see why you should make straight for my bed when you get drunk," he said disagreeably.

"Don't worry—no designs on you. I didn't even know it was your room." I was surprised and thoroughly embarrassed when I finished this statement with a loud hiccup.

"Do you mean to say that you were too drunk to know where you were?"

"I guess so," I said and was suddenly very much ashamed of myself. I had never been really drunk before in my life, and now I had to go and disgrace myself in front of Allan. "It was all your fault, anyway," I said resentfully. "You wouldn't mix the drinks for me, and I've never had to mix drinks and I don't know how."

"You certainly don't," he agreed emphatically. "I can still feel the one you handed me."

I stood up to go, and then I remembered the black paw and sat down again quickly. "I'm not going upstairs—I can't. There's an animal up there."

He looked at me for a moment in silence, and then he asked mildly, "Have you ever had d.t.s?"

"Listen," I said furiously, "I had never been drunk in my life, until I came to this house—and it would drive anyone to drink. As for the animal, I saw its paw, and it was quite clear in the light from the bathroom. And I didn't have to see that paw to know that there's an animal in the house, either."

"Where did you see it? On the third floor?"

I nodded.

"And yet I'm quite sure that there is no animal in the house."

"Oh yeah?" I said and sneered it. "Then there's a very healthy ghost of one." I told him about the marks I had seen and the condition of the Bible, and I finished triumphantly: "When a chair rocks by itself I think the most sensible explanation is that an animal has just leaped off it."

"You're in no condition to give sensible explanations just now," he said. "Why the devil didn't you tell me all this before?"

"You wouldn't listen to me—ever. You kept telling me to get out and stop bothering you."

He said, "Hmm," and stood up. "Think I'll go up and have another look at that Bible."

He went out of the room, and I followed close at his heels. He did not notice me until he was halfway up the stairs, when he turned and told me, in a fierce whisper, to go back. I shook my head stubbornly, and he breathed a few lurid curses before we both proceeded upward.

When we got to Alice's room Allan turned on the light and closed the door. The room was in the same state of confusion, and he shook his head and murmured, "Who could possibly have done this? And why?"

I said, "Oh—I meant to tell you. It was Hattie."

He turned to me sharply and repeated, "Hattie!"

"Yes. I thought you might not want the others to know, so I didn't say anything. But I know she did it."

I told him all about Hattie's visit to the fourth floor, and he said, frowning, "Then she was looking for something and presumably found it on the roof. Sounds a bit absurd."

"I wouldn't know," I said airily. "I'm just telling you what I saw."

"I'll have a talk with Hattie later," he said thoughtfully, and I found myself feeling sorry for Hattie.

He went over to the Bible and examined it carefully, and then he straightened and admitted, "Looks as though it had been chewed all right."

"Let's see if we can find that animal," I said, glancing uneasily over my shoulder.

"What kind of an animal is it?" he asked abruptly.

"I don't know."

"You must have some idea," he said impatiently. "Was it a giraffe?"

"I guess it's either a cat or a dog. Something like that."

"All right, we'll have a look."

He searched the entire floor, with the exception of the storage rooms. The front room with the open window was given a very thorough going over, and he ended up by leaning out of the window and carefully examining the surroundings as far as he could reach. He backed in again, his head and shoulders wet from the rain, and said, "It's quite impossible; there simply is not any hiding place. Are you quite sure Hattie found something there?"

"I've already told you what I saw. She was tucking something into the front of her dress when she turned away from that window."

He shrugged. "Come on, we're going down. And be as quiet as you can."

On the third floor he went straight to my bedroom and turned on the light. He gave the room a brief search and then told me to go to bed. "There's nothing here now, and no one is likely to disturb you. It's nearly morning."

It didn't look or feel like nearly morning, but I noticed that it was five o'clock, so I nodded dispiritedly and watched him walk out of my room and down the stairs.

After he had gone I noticed that the bathroom was in darkness, and because I was still a bit tight I walked boldly in and turned on the light. The tub was empty.

I went back to my room and realized, after a bit of thought, that the bathroom had been dark when Allan and I crept up to the top floor. Evidently, then, the light had been turned off and the tub drained at some time since I had seen the black paw and before Allan and I had gone up to Alice's room.

But why? What was it all about? And why had I ever allowed myself to be persuaded to set foot into this madhouse?

I was too nervous to sleep, and my head was aching, so I decided to go to the second-floor bathroom and get some aspirin—and perhaps to the kitchen, after that, for some coffee. At least Bill would be there, and Bill was better than being alone

On the second floor I heard the sound of subdued voices, and after a moment I realized that it was Hattie and Allan. I reflected that it was exactly like him to wake her at this hour in the morning when he had something on his mind. I moved over to the keyhole and glued my ear.

Hattie was in tears. "You gotta believe me," she sobbed. "I can't tell you anything different than the truth. I was looking for that emerald ring George had. He promised it to me a hundred times and always said it would be mine when he died."

"There was no mention of an emerald ring in the will," Allan said curtly.

"Well—no, he always made out it belonged to Alice, but he didn't keep it up in her room, because I went up once and looked. Then I found out he kept it on him, but now I can't find it. It must be around somewhere, and it's mine. I got a right to what's mine."

"If he had such a thing the chances are he pawned it," Allan said indifferently. "You'd better go through his pawn tickets."

Hattie received this in silence, and after a moment Allan went on: "But what was it you found on the roof and tucked into the front of your dress?"

She gave an outraged little shriek and cried, "What do you mean, Allan Barton? I found nothing anywhere."

"It's no use, Hattie," he said and sounded bored. "You were seen, and you were tucking something into the front of your dress."

"Seen?" she repeated shrilly. "How could I have been seen? Anyway, I didn't— Listen, if you had some damned spy trailing after me, you can tell him I was merely scratching myself."

I heard Allan laugh, and I laughed myself, quietly.

"All right, Hattie," he said after a moment. "We'll continue this in the morning—with Detective Hatton."

I wended my way at that point, because I did not want to be caught wandering around after the master had more or less tucked me in. I let the aspirin go for the time being and went on down to the kitchen.

The light was on, but Bill was not there, and I decided not to search for him, since he was probably within call if I needed him. I made coffee, and as soon as the smell was strong enough it drew Bill to my side. He accepted a cup and asked why I was up and about at five in the morning.

"I can't sleep," I explained, relaxing over the hot drink.

Bill shook his head sadly. "You young girls—there's no tellin' you. You ought to be very careful with them rich fellas. You dive in up to your necks, and then you find all that glitters ain't gold."

"I don't care whether it's gold or not," I said, "as long as it glitters."

Bill was shocked and said so. He gave me a lecture that lasted for fully ten minutes, and I began to wonder what had happened to his modern ideas about married women going out with other men.

I left him after we had finished our coffee, and since my headache was better and dawn breaking, I went all the way up to my room. The rain was drumming steadily against my window, but the room was gray, and I felt relaxed enough to get to sleep. I put the light on, searched the room and then closed the door, put the light out again and got into bed.

I stretched my aching body and had just got my head comfortable on the pillow, when I heard the soft pad of footsteps passing my door.

CHAPTER TWENTY-FIVE

I WAS instantly wide awake again and rigid with fear. The footsteps had been quiet and sounded like someone walking without shoes. I waited for a moment and then got out of bed and crept to the door. Jennie was hurrying past as I peeped out, and I pulled the door wide and whispered, "What's the matter?"

She gave a little jump and turned around with her finger to her lips. "Hush! It's Mr. Keith. He got away before I could stop him." She went on, and I turned back for my wrapper and slippers.

She was making a helpless and frantic search of the second floor when I caught up with her, and she whimpered, "My God! What can I do? I've lost him."

"What's wrong with him?" I asked curiously.

"He's walking in his sleep."

"Well, come on," I said wearily. "He can't have got far. You look around here, and I'll go downstairs."

"You're a good girl, Ellen," she said gratefully. "If you find him, just lead him gently upstairs again—don't wake him."

I nodded and went on down the back stairs. I looked through the kitchen and the dining room and then went to the front hall and the drawing room and study, but I did not find him—and Bill was missing too.

I went to the sitting room last of all, and as I entered by one door I caught a glimpse of Mr. Keith leaving by another. He went swiftly through the dining room and into the back hall, while I stumbled along, trying to catch up with him. I thought he was making for the kitchen, but when he reached the lobby he turned abruptly and went down into the cellar.

I hesitated, shivering with cold and nerves, but in the end I forced myself to go down after him.

The cellar was dark, and I had no idea where to look for the light switch. I stood at the foot of the stairs, straining my eyes into the blackness, and completely at a disadvantage, since he knew the cellar and I did not.

I had decided to go back and get Jennie, when I was frozen to the spot by the sound of his voice. He spoke in a slurred, thick jumble of words, and only bits here and there came out clearly.

"I must—must find the solution—tomorrow. I must—"

He became unintelligible for a while, and then he said clearly, "Whoever shoots straight. I know who shoots straight. I know—I—" The words trailed into silence, and I could hear him working at something and panting a little.

I took a few cautious steps forward and saw the tall, vague outline of him. He was busy at the woodpile, and as far as I could see in the gloom, he appeared to be piling the wood higher.

I was afraid to go near him, and in the end I went up and told Jennie. She hurried down with me, switched on the cellar light and soon had him gently by the arm. She guided him all the way up to their bedroom, and as far as I could see, following behind, he never woke up.

Jennie was limp with relief. "I'm so glad he didn't wake. He gets an awful fright if he wakes up while he's walking, and it's bad for his heart." She had picked up a long piece of string that was lying on the bed and showed it to me. "He must have slipped out of the knot, because I didn't feel much of a pull, and he was away out the door before I got my eyes open. By the time I got the string off my toe and into my dressing gown, he was gone."

I yawned, and she shooed me off to bed and closed her door. It was quite light and close on six o'clock, and I felt that I could sleep for a week. I turned around, went back to Jennie's door and whispered, "Hey!"

"What is it?"

"Five dollars if you let me sleep till noon."

I heard her gasp, and she said, "Caesar's ghost, girl! Where do you get all that money?"

I did not bother to answer or to listen any more. I knew I had sold her, and I went straight to bed and to sleep.

Jennie woke me promptly at twelve noon and had much to say about how I could possibly sloth the morning hours away like this, and where was I getting all the money from, anyway? Five dollars for this, and five dollars for that.

I yawned, paid her the five dollars and began to dress.

She pocketed the money and then sniffed around to see if she could catch an odor of indecency. It was all highly suspicious, she said, and her conscience told her she ought to go straight to Mr. Allan about it.

"Jennie," I said, "your nose would be more beautiful if you didn't keep it stretched and quivering from morning until night. Lord McNab left me a nice hatful of money when he died. I don't have to work, but I think people are happier when they're busy. I do not approve of idle women who spend their lives in hotels, simply living on pleasure."

"It just ain't natural," Jennie interrupted firmly. "It don't ring true—anyone working when they don't have to. Why don't you take care of your money and buy a chicken farm, or something like that?"

"I loathe chickens," I said cheerfully. "Housemaiding is the only work that appeals to me."

She shook her head for a while, until a possible explanation occurred to her. "Maybe you're looking for a husband?" she suggested, brightening. "Yeah, I guess that's it. Well—I'll be getting along. You hurry now."

I did not hurry. I felt that the five-spot should take me right up to lunch, and I dressed leisurely, gave care and attention to my face and hair and even looked out of the window at the rain for a while. But habit is an insidious thing, and I had become so accustomed to hurrying that I got downstairs fifteen minutes before lunch time, anyway.

Jennie was sulky because she had had to set the table herself, but Mr. Keith brushed her aside and took me in hand. He made me go to the cellar with him and search the woodpile.

"Jennie has told me about last night," he explained, "and I am inclined to think that my subconscious mind was at work. I have searched exhaustively for that gun, but I never thought of going through the woodpile. We must do so at once."

"Can't you—what about Oliver?" I said feebly. "I'll get all dirty."

He spared a frown for such foolishness and explained patiently, "Oliver has taken Miss Hattie out for the day, and of course Bill's sleeping, since he was up all night."

"So was I," I groaned, but Mr. Keith was already methodically moving the logs.

We shifted the entire pile, but the gun was not there. We found nothing except three spiders and the bottom half of a small gray cardboard box. I picked the box up and shook it and then used it to shoo the spiders away.

Mr. Keith was badly disappointed, but his faith in his subconscious was not entirely shaken. "We simply have not interpreted it properly yet," he said unhappily. "There must be a clue of some sort. I am convinced that I did not come straight here in my sleep for nothing. I must think it over; I shall spend the afternoon in thought, and I am sure that it will come to me."

We returned to the kitchen, and Mr. Keith repeated to Jennie that he intended to spend the afternoon in thought. She nodded solemn agreement, and I found myself wondering what his duties actually were—aside from waiting on the table with my help.

Allan and Ross were at lunch, but Hattie did not appear. I was not required for service in the dining room, but I found much to occupy me in the serving pantry, and I heard Allan ask Mr. Keith where Hattie and Oliver had gone.

"Miss Hattie did not say, sir. She merely said that she would need Oliver for the day."

Mr. Keith presently came through the swinging door and gently laid his ear against the crack. I lingered close behind him, busily cleaning silver with a dry dish towel and no polish.

"What in the name of God is she up to now?" we heard Allan say.

"Nefarious business of some sort," Ross said indifferently. "She has no money, and—cause and effect—she no longer has Oliver. Today's expedition is probably an effort to draw him back into the fold."

"I thought I'd fixed that," Allan said in an annoyed voice. "I'll spike her guns for her, if she tries it. Damn the woman, anyway. She ought to have more pride than to force me to warn my chauffeur to stay away from my sister-in-law."

"Oh hell, be your age," Ross said, laughing. "Why shouldn't Hattie play around with your chauffeur if she happens to like him?"

"She can elope with him, and I'll send her my blessing and a pickle fork," Allan replied, "but this is neither the time nor the place. George murdered—and barely under the ground. In any case, Oliver was simply out for whatever money he could get, and now that he knows she has none he'll probably leave her strictly alone. She'll get over it, and then I'm going to fire Oliver."

"Good enough," Ross said amiably. "This job's no good to him, anyway. No rich women. I wonder if I'm handsome enough to go into that business—plucking rich women? Easy work, and the hours are not long."

"Oh, shut up," said Allan, and there was a faint hint of distaste in his voice.

"You're no hero to me," Ross said equably. "After all, I haven't been divorced by a woman."

"No women ever married you, either."

"I'm too shrewd," said Ross, "to get hooked."

"The sort of frump I've seen you with in town," Allan replied, "would make no greater demand on you than a cup of coffee at the automat."

Jennie came into the service pantry at that point and broke it up. "Mr. Keith, come quickly," she whispered. "I've found the gun!"

CHAPTER TWENTY-SIX

MR. KEITH and I tore ourselves away from the dining-room door and ran to the kitchen, where Jennie stood brandishing the gun in her hand.

"Drop it! Drop it at once," Mr. Keith cried excitedly.

Jennie dropped it as though it had burned her, and it fell with a loud clatter onto the table. I closed my eyes and hunched my shoulders, expecting it to go off, but nothing happened, so I cautiously opened my eyes again.

Jennie was looking at Mr. Keith with a scared expression.

"Do you realize, woman, that you have ruined whatever fingerprints might have been on it?" he demanded sternly.

Jennie relaxed. "Oh no," she said, relieved. "Crooks wear gloves these days—always. I read it somewhere."

Mr. Keith turned his back on her and went to the dining room to get Allan. They returned to the kitchen, followed by Ross, and after Allan had examined the gun he glanced at Jennie and asked where it had been found.

She began confidently, "I went in the—" and then stopped, unhappily twisting her apron through her fingers, while her face flushed darkly. She made another try, with her eyes on the floor. "I left my soap in the—in there," and indicated the small washroom and toilet that was opposite the cellar stairs. "So I thought I might as well wash my hands in there, since the soap was there, anyway."

Allan stirred impatiently, and she finished it in a hurry: "The gun was under that telephone book in the corner. The book didn't quite cover it, and that's how I saw it."

Ross and I were both grinning happily at Jennie's desperate attempt to conceal the fact that she ever answered nature's call, but Mr. Keith was grave, and Allan frowning thoughtfully. They went into the washroom and looked it over, and then Allan came back, wrapped the gun in a kitchen towel and took it off, with Ross and Mr. Keith trailing him.

After they had gone I inspected the washroom myself. I found nothing unusual, except the telephone book. I knew that the kitchen telephone was supplied with a book that hung on a nail directly beneath it. I advanced to the corner of the little room, where the book lay on a small shelf, and saw that it was dated the previous year.

I backed into the kitchen, where Jennie was preparing our lunch, and asked, "What is that old telephone book doing in the washroom, anyway?"

"I keep it there for emergency," she explained in a low, one-woman-to-another voice. "Once in a while I forget to order toilet rolls, and I have to take the roll in there and the one in our bathroom upstairs to supply the family. So I keep a couple of old telephone books, just to have handy."

I laughed until Jennie began to eye me uneasily. I knew myself that I was a bit hysterical, but the disapproving face of Mr. Keith, returning to the kitchen, brought me around. I drew a long breath, dried my eyes and sat down at the table.

As soon as I had finished my lunch I stood up and began to maneuver myself out of the kitchen so that I could have a cigarette.

Jennie fixed me with small, suspicious eyes and asked, "Where are you going?"

"To the toilet," I said brazenly.

She dropped her eyes, silenced by such indelicacy in front of Mr. Keith. I picked up the small cardboard box that I had found under the woodpile, to be used as an ashtray, and stepped into the lobby, closing the door firmly behind me. There were no chairs there or in the back hall, so I walked through into the front hall. I fished the cigarettes from my bosom, where I was forced to keep them, owing to a lack of pockets in maids' uniforms, and seating myself comfortably, I proceeded to smoke.

But there was never any peace in that house. Allan suddenly appeared from the dining room, and I could see by his expression that I was heading into trouble again.

He came and stood directly in front of me. "What the hell are you doing?"

"It would be more sensible to ask me how I feel," I said, flicking ash into the dusty little box. "You can see what I'm doing. I am smoking. Any child of five could have told you."

"You can save that flip talk for the kitchen. When you answer me you'll watch your tongue and your manners. Now why are you sitting smoking here, in the hall, when I've told you that sitting and smoking are to be done in your own private quarters?"

"My own quarters are never privy," I said bitterly, "but I did think this hall might be. I was under the impression that you and Ross—Mister—had gone upstairs."

I steeled myself for the terrific berating that I fully expected, but it did not come. Allan was staring at the gray cardboard box in my hand.

"Where did you get that?" he demanded.

"In the woodpile. I don't think," I said politely, "that there are any more there, but you may have this one if it appeals to you."

"Give it to me," he said abruptly and took it out of my hand.

He examined it carefully, turning it around and upside down and dropping all the ashes onto the floor. I stooped down and blew at them vigorously, so that I would not have to come back later and clean them up.

He presently glanced at me and said irritably, "Get up off the floor. Where's the lid?"

"Of that box?" I asked, dusting off my knees. "I don't know."

"It's the box which used to contain bullets for that gun," he said, half to himself.

I stared at him. "Then maybe Mr. Keith's subconscious had the right idea, after all."

"What are you talking about?"

I told him all about Mr. Keith and the woodpile, and without a word of thanks he turned his back on me and made for the kitchen. I followed, determined not to miss anything.

Jennie and Mr. Keith were still sipping the black, bitter brew that they called tea, but they abandoned their cups and sprang to attention.

"Look here, Keith," Allan said, "don't you recognize this box?"

Mr. Keith examined the thing carefully and said, "Why, yes sir. It's part of the box in which you kept bullets for the gun."

Allan said, "Yes. Then why didn't you tell me about it as soon as you found it in the woodpile?"

Mr. Keith blinked and stammered, "I beg your pardon, sir?"

I insinuated an explanation that I had found the thing myself and had absentmindedly kept it in my hand, with no idea that it had any importance. Mr. Keith, with very little alteration in his expression, silently threatened me with retribution. When he spoke, however, he merely said courteously, "You should have told me about it, Ellen."

"Detective Hatton is due here at any moment, Keith," Allan said impatiently. "I think we'd better search that woodpile again, and the entire cellar as well. Come on."

They departed, and I turned to assist Jennie with the dishes. Once I went to the top of the cellar stairs and listened. I could hear various sounds of physical labor, and I kept absolutely quiet, for fear I'd be called down to give a hand.

Mr. Keith delivered himself of a bright idea while I stood there. "Do you know what I think, sir? It seems to me the other bullets must be up in the kitchen somewhere."

"Why?" Allan asked in a muffled voice.

"Well—somewhere handy to the cellar door, anyway. Why, it's plain, sir, that that gun was placed in the washroom only recently. I expect it was originally hidden in the woodpile, and whoever put it there heard of my having gone straight to that spot in my sleep. It must have been hastily moved from there, in case I should search through the wood when I was awake—as I did. You see, sir, your subconscious mind works in a peculiar fashion, and mine must have told me that the woodpile had not been properly searched."

"Perhaps," Allan said, obviously with scant patience for Mr. Keith's subconscious. "You feel pretty sure then that the gun was not hidden in the washroom all along?"

"Pretty sure, sir. I am convinced that it would have been discovered before this. Jennie cleans that washroom every day, and if I may say so, Jennie never goes around things—she goes under."

"All right," said Allan. "Let's go up and look around."

They came up and looked around until Jennie was on the verge of apoplexy. They poked into flour and sugar bins, tea and coffee canisters, and they even went carefully through the inside of the oven.

Jennie, shifting from one foot to the other and watching her neat and immaculate arrangements being thrown into confusion, kept repeating unhappily, "I'm sure there's nothing here."

I used the opportunity to sneak out of the kitchen and get away, since I knew that Jennie would have plenty of work for me if I hung around.

I met Ross in the hall, heading for the kitchen, and he asked, "What's going on?"

I said briefly, "They're looking for things," and brushed past him.

I went up to the third floor and then perversely wished that I had stayed downstairs where it was more cheerful and there were people about me.

I stretched out on my bed and lit a cigarette, but I could not relax. Fear grew in me as the minutes passed, and at last I got slowly off the bed and crushed out my cigarette.

As I stood there, tense with nervousness, I heard the high, snarling wail of a cat.

CHAPTER TWENTY-SEVEN

I FLEW DOWN the stairs in a panic. It was not that I was afraid of a cat in the ordinary way, but in my mind this one was composed of an eerie cry, a black paw and two separate and single paw marks.

I bumped into Allan on the second floor and clutched at him with a little gasp. "Quickly! That animal—it's a cat!"

"Not really!" he said and walked away from me toward his room.

"But it's in the house," I said desperately. "It yelled—I heard it."

"Oh, save it for Jennie," he said crossly. "You're always coming to me with tales, and none of them is worth a damn."

"All right," I said furiously. "But it's a pity you didn't listen to me when I tried to tell you about your sister."

He stopped and gave me a curious, silent look, and then he turned abruptly and started up the stairs to the third floor. I followed him and could not help feeling rather sorry that I had mentioned Franny.

When we reached the third floor he turned to me and asked briefly, "Where were you when you heard this noise?"

"In my room there. But the wail came from upstairs."

"Are you quite certain that it was not outside?"

"Absolutely sure," I insisted. "It came from the floor above."

We went up to the top floor, and Allan directed me to stand at the head of the stairs while he searched the rooms. "Keep your eyes open and yell if it runs out of any of these doors."

I stood there, nervously alert, while he searched, but nothing happened. Once he came out into the hall and asked if I knew who had shut the window.

"What window?" I asked.

"The window that's usually open—the one where Hattie found something."

"Oh. No. I don't know anything about it." I had no very clear memory about that window being either open or shut. I felt that someone could have closed it in front of my eyes, and I would not have remembered.

Allan searched carefully until he came to the storage rooms. He glanced casually into each of them and shut their doors carefully. "It would take hours to search those two rooms. There might easily be a cat in one of them, but it won't be able to get out with the doors closed, and I'll speak to Detective Hatton about it." He went into Alice's room for a final look around, and while he was there I caught sight of Bill pressed against the wall at the foot of the stairs, with his ears yearning upward. Allan came into the hall again, and I said loudly, "Darling, it's wonderful to have you to myself—just for these few little minutes."

Allan stared at me, and I grinned and pointed down the stairs. However, he apparently was not in the mood, for he muttered, "Shut up" under his breath and brushed past me.

When we got down to the third floor Bill was carefully examining a crack in the wall. Allan told him about the cat, said, "I want you to find it," and went off downstairs.

Bill watched him disappear, and then said in an injured voice, "I ain't no dogcatcher."

"It's a cat," I said helpfully.

"Listen," said Bill, "if he wants to get rid of livestock in the house, why don't he put poison around?"

"But, Bill, this is a valuable cat—probably worth thousands. Maybe you'll get a reward if you find it."

He scratched his head and murmured, "No kiddin'?"

"Everybody is looking for it," I urged, "and if you find it—"

"Where is it?" asked Bill slowly.

"Somewhere on the top floor."

"O.K., I'll run up and get it. You wait here, baby, and give me the high sign if the boss comes along."

I nodded, and he went up the stairs. I stood guard until Jennie happened along, when I was dragged down to the kitchen. There was nothing I could do about it but hope that Bill would not get into trouble.

I was worked until nearly five, when Jennie made a pot of tea and graciously allowed me to sit down with her and have a cup, probably because I had been a good girl all the afternoon.

Oliver came in while we were sitting at the table and delivered himself of some gossip. Hattie had spent the day in New York, and after telling Oliver that she did not believe in mourning, had bought a complete wardrobe of summer clothes. "Every color in the goddam rainbow," Oliver said, leaning against the sink and chewing on a toothpick.

Jennie was surprised. "I thought they closed all the charge accounts on her after what happened last year."

"What happened last year?" I asked.

"Oh, she ran up a lot of bills, and Mr. Allan had to pay them because nobody else could. He closed out all his accounts then, but I guess he let her get that mourning outfit."

Oliver said, "Yeah—but getta loada this. She paid spot cash for everything today."

Jennie nearly dropped her cup. "What!" she yelled.

"Fact." Oliver shifted the toothpick. "I been tryin' to break it up with her, and she's been sore as hell at me, but today she opens up. Nothing won't do but I got to go in all the stores with her and carry the packages. She made me eat lunch with her, and she pays everything off a wad big enough to choke you. I got the car loaded like a Mack truck, and all I gotta do now is carry all them damn things up to her room."

"Well, there's something queer going on," Jennie said grimly. "All I know is she ain't had any money for weeks—she even owes me five dollars." She stopped suddenly, and her little eyes gleamed. "Maybe this is a good time to remind her about it."

She went off in a hurry, and Oliver straightened up with a gusty sigh. "Well, see ya later, babe. I gotta clear the junk outa that car."

I relaxed comfortably over my tea and came to the conclusion that Hattie had found money on the roof. I finished my tea and ducked out of the kitchen, hoping to steer clear of Jennie for a while. I roamed the halls, half hoping to run into Ross, and instead I nearly ran into Detective Hatton. He was coming out of the drawing room, and I had to slip outside the front door in order to miss him. I waited until I saw him head for the kitchen, and then I went quietly into the drawing room.

I heard Allan and Ross talking in the study, and I opened the door and walked straight in. They were both drinking, and two minutes' observation told me that they had been drinking for some time.

I said, "Hello," sat comfortably in an armchair and pulled out my cigarettes. "Do give me a drink," I added, keeping my eyes carefully away from Allan, and feeling conscious of a ridiculous fear that he was about to box my ears.

Ross stood up, bowed low and began to mix me a drink. Allan gave me a cold stare and said, "I promise you that your impertinence is going to get a taking down."

"Pay him no heed," Ross said amiably. "He's been playing purse-holding head of the house for so long that *he* isn't even human."

I said fervently, "Oh, I know."

"Get out of that chair at once and go back to the kitchen," Allan snapped.

"If I do decide to get out of this chair," I said carefully, "I most certainly shall not go back to the kitchen. I shall go in search of Detective Hatton."

"Blackmail, by the sound of it," said Allan indifferently. "Go ahead—spill it."

"No hurry," I murmured, easing myself into a more comfortable position. "I want a rest, and after I've spilled it I shall be sent back to the scullery."

"Without a doubt," said Allan ominously, "you will—wherever the scullery may be. In the meantime, would you care to have afternoon tea served? And if it won't irk you too much to wait, shall I go and put on a clean collar?"

Ross handed me my drink. "Round one," he observed. "I don't know why you try to fight her off, Allan. She's the cutest little trick, and she'll get you in the end, anyhow."

I choked over the drink, and when I came up for air I saw that they were both laughing, and I was suddenly furious. "It's too bad," I said nastily, "that you're both so stuck for women that you have to pretend the scullery maid is after you."

"What is a scullery maid?" Ross interrupted. "Does she know what it means? Or is she just using it?"

Allan said, "I'm getting bored." And I added, "Me too."

Ross laughed, and I suddenly sat up straight. "I could wipe that laugh off your face with a few words."

"All right, little one, I'm all ears."

"Then listen. The money you hid in this house has been invested in a new summer wardrobe for Hattie."

The laugh disappeared like magic, and Ross's expression became pure fury. The two of them demanded details, and I told what I knew. When I had finished Ross stormed out of the room, apparently on his way to Hattie.

I started to follow and was pulled back by Allan. "Here, have another drink and keep your snooping little nose out of this."

I accepted a glass from him and sat down. He threw himself into a chair facing me and said unexpectedly, "Now I want to tell you something. You're to stop sending me those love letters."

CHAPTER TWENTY-EIGHT

I SPRANG up from my chair and glared at him. "What do you mean? How dare you accuse me of sending you love letters?"

"Notes," he corrected.

"I don't care what you call them. I never—"

He got up from his chair and gagged me with his hand over my mouth. "All right, you didn't write the damn things," he said in a low voice. "No need to let the whole house know about it."

He pushed me down into my chair again and pulled his chair close to mine. He sat down and pulled the notes out of his pocket.

I saw that there were two of them, and the first one said, "Darling, would like to see you tonight. Ellen."

"I found that one around lunch time," Allan said. "It was in my bedroom, propped up against a book on the bureau.. The other was in the study here, standing against a book on the desk.

I looked at the second note, which read, "My dear, will you please meet me in the front room on the top floor tonight at about twelve o'clock? Have something very important to tell you. Ellen."

I stared at the thing with a gone feeling in my stomach, for the handwriting was exactly like mine.

Allan was watching me, and I turned to him and said earnestly, "I did not write these notes, and I know nothing about them. I think someone must be trying to get you onto the fourth floor tonight. You can tell yourself that I didn't write them, since I wouldn't sign myself 'Ellen' to you."

He nodded. "That had occurred to me," he admitted. "Is the handwriting at all like your own?"

"It's exactly like my own," I said faintly.

"Are you sure then?"

"I didn't write them," I broke in impatiently. "It's a clever copy."

"In that case, from what were they copied? Is there a specimen of your handwriting in your bedroom? Or anywhere else in the house?"

I stared at him in sudden fear. I was pretty sure that there was no specimen of my handwriting in the house. I had brought nothing of that kind with me, and I could not remember having written a line since I had come.

"Why, I don't—I can't think of anything," I whispered. "But there must be something I must have forgotten. Because I did not write those notes myself."

He stood up. "All right. Now I want you to go straight up to your room and make a thorough search for anything that might have your handwriting on it. You may dig up something."

I nodded and pulled myself out of the chair. I was surprised to see that Allan was a bit unsteady on his feet, although I had seen him take several drinks; and supposed that he must have had several before I came.

"Just a minute," he said as I turned to go. "At dinner tonight you are to touch my hand—unostentatiously, you understand but make very sure that everyone else sees it."

"Why?" I asked, staring.

"I want everyone to know that you still love me."

"But Bill won't be at dinner," I stammered. "Or Detective Hatton."

He said, "My dear scullery maid, your wit is a little dim. I want the writer of those notes to think he has put it over and that I will certainly keep the twelve-o'clock tryst. As a matter of fact, I shall squeeze your hand by way of return."

"Hot dog!"

He fixed me with a cold eye. "Dinner is the best possible time, since everyone will be there except Jennie and Oliver, and Keith will bring them the news a good deal faster than it was brought from Aix to Ghent."

"But—surely you're not going up to the fourth floor at twelve tonight?"

"Yes, I am," he said. "And get this. You're to go to your room and stay there, and if you so much as poke your nose outside the door I'll horsewhip you."

I shook my head and started for the door. With my hand on the knob I turned and asked, "Does Ross know about these notes? I mean, is that why he inferred I was trying to get you?"

"No one knows about them but you and myself—and whoever wrote them. That is, of course, if someone else did write them. I shouldn't want to bet on it."

I turned around and opened my mouth, but he closed it for me. "I know, I know. You certainly didn't write those notes. Now get going, before Jennie reports you missing."

I went through the drawing room and the entrance hall and up the front stairs without meeting anyone or seeing any paw marks, and I was on the lookout for both. I noticed that the stairs were thick with dust, and wondered why Jennie had not smelled it out, even though she invariably used the back stairs herself.

The second floor was loud with the sound of voices from Hattie's room, and my manners had sunk so low that I did not think twice about sneaking over and putting my ear against the panel.

Hattie's voice was piercing and hysterical, and she was asking Ross if he didn't suppose that she had any relatives who could help her out? After all, her relatives were not in the gutter, and why shouldn't they rally to her aid when she was destitute?

She paused, of necessity, to get her breath, and Ross asked her, with a sort of steely calm, which one of her relatives had sent her the money and when had it arrived.

"None of your business," Hattie shouted. "You can keep your nose out of my affairs."

Ross must have been right at the door, because he suddenly came out into the hall, and I had to back up hastily. I said, "Sorry," in some confusion.

Ross smiled and asked mildly, "Why?"

"For eavesdropping," I explained and noticed that his fury seemed to have evaporated. "Where did you have that money hidden?" I added.

"Why do you want to know?" he asked, grinning down at me. "Are you going to detect out the truth for me?"

Perhaps I blushed then; I don't know.

"I'll tell you," Ross went on, "if you'll do me a favor."

"Anything that I can," I agreed.

He brought his left hand from behind his back, and I saw that he held one of Hattie's large cheap purses. "Now we'll open it," he murmured, "and see how much of my money—if any—is left." He fumbled through the thing, and at last brought out a roll of bills that counted up to a hundred and thirty-five dollars.

"Hell!" he muttered. "The dizzy cluck has spent more than half of it."

"I'm sorry," I said, shaking my head.

"Oh well." He shrugged. "This is better than losing the lot. What I want you to do is this. Go in there and ask her if she wants a cocktail, or something, and put this purse back on the end of the bed, from where I snitched it. Only don't let her see you doing it."

I said, "All right," rather doubtfully, and he smiled and pinched my chin.

"The money was hidden in a break in the plaster in that cupboard under the front stairs," he said and took himself off.

I clutched nervously at Hattie's purse, and after a minute or two to rally my courage, I took a long breath and walked into Hattie's bedroom. The thing was easy, after all. Hattie stood at the window with her back to the room, muttering to herself and angrily banging the cord of the window shade against the pane. Apparently she did not hear me, so I put the purse on the bed and crept out again.

I went straight up to my room and made a thorough search, but I found no specimen of my handwriting whatsoever. I sat down to think it over, but I did not get very far before Mr. Keith came rapping at my door.

I called, "Come in," rather absently, and Mr. Keith came in.

"Oh, there you are," he said, raising his eyebrows. "Wherever have you been?"

"All over," I said shortly.

"All over where?" asked Mr. Keith, looking puzzled.

"All over the house."

"I have searched the house," he said reprovingly, "very carefully. I don't see how you could have eluded me."

"I was playing hide-and-seek with you," I said, yawning. "Whenever I saw you coming I hid."

"Did you, indeed?" he asked with quiet menace.

I stood up. "Come on. I dare say you want me to set the table."

"I dare say," said Mr. Keith, following me down the stairs. He added quietly, "I am afraid you will be obliged to work after dinner tonight, since your work has been neglected the entire day."

"I should gladly do just that," I said airily, "only I'm afraid I'm going to have a toothache tonight."

Mr. Keith said levelly and in a voice full of meaning, "We shall see."

I shrugged and realized that I had largely lost my awe of Mr. Keith.

Just before dinner was served I stepped to the kitchen mirror and did a bit of titivating.

Jennie glared at me and asked, "What do you think you're doing now?"

"Why not?" said Oliver. "Coupla big boys in there."

I winked at Oliver, said, "Oh, you fresh thing!" and swaggered into the dining room. I was suffering a little from stage fright, but I was determined to give a good performance. I did too. It was drama of high excellence, and I had the attention of the entire audience. The thing was done in a flat silence, which was broken only when I dropped a spoon in my nervousness.

Mr. Keith made the kitchen before I did, and by the time I got there I could see that he had told all.

Jennie stared at me with her mouth open, but she did not speak until Mr. Keith had returned to the dining room.

"You forward hussy," she said then. "I heard what you just did in there."

"What did I do?" I asked conversationally.

"Making up to Mr. Allan! You're a pretty girl, Ellen, but let me warn you that mixing in with the gentry will bring you to no good end."

"When I come to the end," I said carelessly, "I don't care whether it's good or bad—so long as it's the end."

Oliver thought that was pretty good, and he slapped his thigh and laughed uproariously. "Snappy thinkin', babe," he said approvingly.

Jennie folded her lips into a thin line, and I returned to the dining room.

When I pushed through the swing door I saw that Mr. Keith was busy drawing the curtains; Allan appeared to be half asleep; Ross had his head under the table, apparently looking for something, and Hattie was dropping a powder into Ross's coffee.

CHAPTER TWENTY-NINE

I DIDN'T LIKE Hattie, so I decided to be on Ross's side. His face appeared again above the table, and he had his napkin in his hand. He glanced at me and grinned. "Thought the thing had got away from me completely. If I were an aristocrat I could anchor it through a buttonhole in my waistcoat and hang onto it."

"Never mind," I said, walking toward him. "I'm quite fond of the bourjoursie myself." I leaned down, breathed into his ear, "Don't drink your coffee," and walked on.

I was conscious of a frigid current emanating from Mr. Keith, but before he could order me into the kitchen to deal with me Hattie got in ahead of him.

"Listen, you. You're getting too darned familiar around here. You're fired. Who do you think you are, anyway? Playing up to all the men."

"I have to work fast in this house," I said pertly, "to get my fair share of them."

Ross was laughing, and Mr. Keith began to walk toward me purposefully. I glanced at Allan and saw, with a sinking feeling, that his eyes were open and he was staring at me. I knew that he was drunk and had supposed that he was more or less in a stupor, but I could see at once that I had misjudged his condition.

He said, "Ellen, you will apologize to Mrs. Barton at once for that remark."

I felt like Elsie Dinsmore, but I decided not to be such a sissy as she was.

"I will not," I said bravely. "I am of the masses, but you cannot make me grovel."

Mr. Keith took a hand at that point. He obviously did not approve of scenes in his perfectly arranged dining room, and he simply walked out into the kitchen, pushing me in front of him. When he got me there he shot his cuffs and prepared to speak.

I turned on him and got in first: "And you can shut up. If I see fit to get into trouble with my employers it's no concern of yours, one way or the other." I sat down and took out a cigarette.

"I had intended to try and save your job for you," Mr. Keith said in a voice of still fury, "even after your impossible behavior of this evening. But now you will undoubtedly have to go."

"Well, thank God for that," I said, lighting my cigarette. "I'll take the first train in the morning, and between now and then I'll have a complete rest."

Jennie gasped, and Mr. Keith turned away without a word and went back into the dining room.

"You are a bold one," Jennie observed with the faintest possible hint of unwilling admiration. "What have you done now?"

"First I made up to Mr. Ross," I said readily, "and Mrs. Hattie gave me hell, so then I was impertinent to her. After that Mr. Allan told me to apologize, and I refused—right to his face."

Jennie shook her head and clicked her tongue several times. "I don't know what in the world makes you carry on like that. However did you keep your place with Lord McNab?"

"Oh well," I said easily, "I understand very well how to handle the aristocracy."

"Are you trying to say that the Bartons are not aristocracy?" Jennie demanded angrily.

"Indeed, they're not. Why, they even have coffee served in the dining room."

"Not when they have guests," Jennie said, still defending her tribe. "We serve coffee in the drawing room when there are guests."

"Yes, but of course, that's just the difference, you see. The McNabs always had coffee in the drawing room."

Jennie wrinkled her brow in an effort to get around that one, and while she was still in the throes, Ross put his head in at the door and said, "Come here a minute, Ellen, will you?"

He drew me into the back hall and waited for a moment, with his hand on my arm, until Hattie, who was climbing the stairs, reached the top. Then he asked, "Why was I not to drink my coffee?"

"Because Hattie had dropped a powder into it," I said simply.

He looked utterly astonished and said, "For God's sake!"

I nodded.

"But—why?"

"I don't know," I said, "because I didn't ask her."

"But I can't understand it. Why on earth should she do a thing like that?"

I offered a suggestion: "Maybe she found that the rest of the money had disappeared from her bag. She'd guess that you had taken it, and probably she wanted to put you out cold so that she could steal it back again."

He said slowly, "That's it—must be. I'll pretend to fall asleep in my room, and when that cheap ham comes in to search I'll give her an appropriate reception."

"She might have noticed that you didn't drink your coffee though," I objected.

"I don't believe so," he said, shaking his head. "I told Keith to take it away, and later she asked me if I had enjoyed it—or some silly remark like that. I told her it was excellent coffee."

"Hattie," I observed, "conducts her intrigues rather crudely."

"You don't though," Ross said, looking down at me. I glanced up and saw that he was faintly smiling. I could see that he was preparing to attempt a gay evening of some sort with me, so I said rather hastily that I had to go.

He pulled me back with a persuasive hand on my arm. "Don't, you're always running away. And I want to kiss you."

"Some other time," I said lightly.

He said, "No—now," and put his arm around me.

I didn't want to kiss him, somehow, so I scuffled away from him, and then I noticed that Allan had come into the hall from the dining room and was leaning against the wall, watching us. He stirred as I looked at him and said, "Ross."

Ross glanced up and said, "Later, my dear fellow. You should not intrude at a time like this."

"Can't help it," said Allan, "it irritates me. You're doing the thing all wrong."

"Maybe," Ross suggested, "you could do better."

Allan shifted away from the wall and advanced on us.

"Certainly I can do better. There's only one technique to be used in kissing a reluctant woman." He took my wrist in a firm grip and explained: "Just turn the lady's wrist slightly, and you can do as you will with her. If the lady shows fight, twist more strongly until she stops kicking." He proceeded to enfold me with his free arm and gave me a long, deliberate kiss.

Ross broke it up. He said hastily, "I see, think I have it now—thanks awfully. I shan't make the same blunder again."

Allan released me, said, "Right," and walked off. He made the front stairs all right and got up by hanging onto the banister all the way.

Ross and I watched him, and Ross said finally, "I'm damned if I see why you prefer him to me. You must admit that he's a bit stuffy."

"Yes," I said helplessly and groping for words. "Stuffy, I guess—but he's not a stuffed shirt."

"What's the distinction?"

"Well—"

"I won't press you," he interrupted kindly, "because you know you're at a loss. In fact, I'll be kind enough to give you a tip. I believe that you can get him if you want him."

"Pooh!" I said loftily. "It's not a matter of whether I can get him—it's a matter of whether he can get me."

"Come off it," Ross said, laughing. "Of course he can get you. And I'll waste enough breath to warn you that living out here in this dusty old tomb is no life for a young girl. Look at Selma."

"What should I do then?"

"Come out and have some fun with me. I have some money now, and your dark-browed he-man will be lying on his bed, sleeping it off, for some time to come."

I couldn't help laughing, and I said, "All right," and then remembered Allan's midnight date on the fourth floor. "Only you'll have to get me back here by twelve."

"Good God!" Ross said. "Twelve?"

"Twelve," I said firmly.

"All right, if you say so, twelve it shall be. Now go and put on your party dress."

"This is it," I said dubiously. "The other is hardly suitable."

"No matter," he said. "Your beauty would ornament a flour sack."

The doorbell pealed in the kitchen, loud and insistent. I made a half step and then remembered that Mr. Keith liked to see for himself who came to the door and why. He appeared almost immediately from the kitchen, and as he passed me, without moving a muscle of his face, he gave me a look that left a bruise.

I heard him open the front door, and there floated back of us the high, excited voice of Mr. Evans. "Good evening, Keith, I must see Mr. Barton—Mr. Allan Barton—immediately. It is most important."

Mr. Keith spoke soothingly, ushered the agitated little man into the sitting room and promised to produce Mr. Barton as speedily as possible.

Ross had slipped into the dining room, as soon as the visitor's voice identified him, with a muttered "Excuse me. I'll have to disappear until the old bore has gone." I hoped, for Ross's sake, that the sliding doors between the two rooms were closed.

Mr. Keith went upstairs, and I returned to the kitchen, where Jennie was sipping tea and Oliver lounged, idly picking his teeth.

I realized that I had not yet had my dinner, so I sat down and pulled the remnants of the meal around me. "Mr. Evans has come to see Mr. Allan," I told them. "He said it was important."

"The half-baked old boob," Oliver observed, without venom.

"He is not any such thing," Jennie protested angrily. "He's a very fine man."

Oliver laughed and stood up. "I'm goin' up to catch some sleep. I gotta do my sleepin' when I get the chance, which ain't often."

He went off, just as Mr. Keith came in.

"I don't quite know what to do," Mr. Keith said in a distressed voice and addressing himself solely to Jennie. "I informed Mr. Allan that Mr. Evans was waiting to see him, and he said he'd be down in a minute and went straight off to sleep again. I roused him and repeated my message, and he—er—requested me to leave the room."

"Told you to get out," I said, making it simpler.

"No one is talking to you, and your remarks are uncalled for," Mr. Keith said icily.

"Be quiet, Ellen," Jennie said in a preoccupied voice. She faced Mr. Keith with a worried frown. "What are we to do? We can't leave Mr. Evans just to sit there."

Mr. Keith shrugged and eased himself into a chair. "I have done my duty, and that is enough."

Jennie stood there for a moment, twisting her apron in her hands, and then she said with decision, "I'll go up—maybe I can manage him. Seems as though I've never known Mr. Allan to get into a condition like this."

She went off, and I was left alone with Mr. Keith. He was seated in the most comfortable chair, and he picked up a newspaper and screened himself behind it. I longed to put a match to it, but was able to control myself.

I finished my dinner and smoked a cigarette in a silence broken only by an occasional rustle from Mr. Keith's newspaper.

Jennie came back after a while, looking pleased with herself. "Well," she said cheerily, "I think I got him going. When I left he was standing in front of the mirror, straightening his tie."

"Good!" said Mr. Keith. "Then as soon as you have cleaned up here we can go upstairs."

Jennie nodded and began to bustle around the disordered kitchen, and I helped as usual. Nothing more had been said about my being fired, and in any case, I knew that Jennie would have to do the work alone if I did not help her. I felt rather generous and high-minded about it, as a matter of fact, and by the time we had finished I had worked myself into such a mellow glow from self-praise that I gave Mr. Keith a charming smile and said, "Good night" to him.

He ignored my overture completely, and I went up the back stairs, shaking my head over him and feeling that he could learn not to be hard and unforgiving from me. I tripped halfway up, which lowered my self-esteem a trifle, and Jennie, directly behind me, laughed and said, "You won't be getting married this year, young lady."

I paused on the second floor to get my breath, and as Jennie and Mr. Keith came abreast of me Hattie poured out of her room, wildly waving her purse around.

"I've been robbed!" she yelled dramatically.

CHAPTER THIRTY

THE THREE OF US stared at her, and it seemed to annoy her. "Well, what are you gaping at?" she yelled. "Get the police at once."

Mr. Keith said, "Yes, madam," and began to mount the stairs to the third floor. "I believe that Bill person is upstairs."

Oliver, descending, passed Mr. Keith and leaned over the banister to inquire, "Who's bein' arrested down here?"

Hattie grabbed at him and began to whine. "Oh, Oliver, come down and help me. I've been robbed, they haven't left me a cent."

Oliver stiffened and muttered, "Too bad," but he remained where he was.

Hattie's eyes began to spark and she said imperiously, "Come here, Oliver; you'll have to stay with me. I can't be alone; I'm too nervous. And I think maybe I'm going to faint."

Oliver walked down the few remaining stairs with obvious reluctance and followed Hattie into her room. Just before the door closed he looked over his shoulder and made a face at Jennie and me. Jennie sighed and began wearily to climb the stairs. "I'm going to bed. It's no concern of mine," she said with patent lack of sympathy for Hattie's plight.

I turned to follow her and was arrested by a loud "psst." I looked up and down the deserted hall and saw nothing human, but another "psst" directed my eye to Ross's door. It was open a crack, and I went over to it and was unceremoniously yanked into the room by Ross himself.

He said, "For God's sake, what is this? We get it doped out that Hattie knows I took what was left of my money and tries to put me to sleep in order to swipe it again—and now we find her having hysterics because she's just discovered the loss." He ran a fretful hand through his hair and added uncomfortably, "Perhaps she was trying to kill me. That powder might have been poison."

I heard Mr. Keith and Bill come down the stairs and listened while they went into Hattie's room. I wondered vaguely whether Bill still had been searching for the elusive animal and felt pity stir within me. He must have wanted the reward pretty badly because, as far as I knew, he had actually missed his dinner.

Ross was saying, "I didn't come out when she made all that fuss just now, because I wanted her to think her damned powder had worked on me. And I'll have to go and lie down now and pretend to sleep, in order to see what she's up to. If she doesn't appear at all I'll take it that the dose was intended to kill me."

I wanted to reassure him, but reason stepped in and prevented me. I whispered, "You don't really think that Hattie—"

"I don't know," Ross said grimly. "But somebody killed George and Franny, and I'm going to keep a sharp eye on that cheap dizzy."

"I guess you'd better," I said slowly.

He looked at me and smiled for the first time. "It means that we can't go out tonight, little one. I'm sorry."

I said, "Not at all; I'm used to it. I've had a date about every night since I've been here, and my legs are aching from standing up on them."

He laughed and said, "I don't believe it."

I opened the door cautiously, said that the coast was clear and slipped out. There seemed to be a convention going on in Hattie's room; I could hear her voice and those of Mr. Keith, Bill and Oliver. I wanted no part in it, so I made for the stairs, but as I was about to start up I caught a glimpse of Allan through his half-opened door, sitting quietly in a chair.

I hesitated, wondering a little what he was doing there and why he was not lying on his bed. I thought of Mr. Evans and wondered if he and Allan had ever connected, or if Allan had merely got as far as the chair and then foundered.

I went quietly into the room, feeling that it was a little hard on Mr. Evans if he were still waiting.

Allan was asleep, and it gave me a certain amount of pleasure to arouse him urgently. He came out of it slowly and asked in a thick mutter, "What in hell do you want now?"

"Did you see Mr. Evans?" I demanded.

"Who?"

"Mr. Evans!" I said, raising my voice.

"Don't shout."

"Listen," I said slowly and distinctly. "Mr. Evans has something very important to tell you, and he's waiting for you in the sitting room."

"Well, why didn't you say so?" He held onto the back of the chair and got slowly to his feet. "Mr. Evans," he said, with dignity. "Yes, of course. I was just on my way down to see him."

"Oh, take off the beard," I said impatiently. "I know you're drunk. And personally, I think it's disgusting."

"Personally," he observed, making for the door, "I think so too. But it's hardly your place to express an opinion."

I followed him out. "Would you care to lean on me, sir? The stairs are ever so treacherous when you're not yourself."

He said, "No, I would not. You might break."

"That wouldn't matter, sir."

"No," he said, "it wouldn't, would it?"

I preceded him down the stairs and hung onto the banister all the way. I did not want him to break his neck, and, even more important, I did not want him to break mine.

We reached the bottom in safety and went along to the sitting room. I was sure that I should presently be dismissed, but I had every intention of eavesdropping in any case.

I was doomed to disappointment, however, since Mr. Evans was not there. Nor was he in the dining room, the drawing room, the study or the kitchen.

We ended our search in the kitchen and stood in the middle of the floor, looking at each other.

"Stupid place to hunt," Allan said sleepily. "Why should he be in the kitchen?"

"He could have been hungry and come here for a bite to eat. You kept him waiting long enough."

"You don't know Mr. Evans, or you would not make so foul a

suggestion. He is a reverend gentleman, and he would not sneak into anyone's kitchen to pilfer food. Sustenance, in all Mr. Evans' holy existence, has been brought to him. I doubt if —"

"All right," I said hastily, "Mr. Evans is too refined to enter a kitchen. Then he must have gone home in a huff because you kept him waiting for so long."

"I'll phone him in the morning," said Allan, losing interest. "I'm going to bed."

"You might better," I agreed mildly.

I followed him out into the hall, where he stopped abruptly. "By God," he said, eying me, "I believe you gave me some lip at dinner."

"I believe I did."

He stared at me for a moment and then said, "I'll attend to that in the morning."

"Sure," I agreed, "if I'm still here. You were asleep at the time, but Hattie fired me."

"You know as well as I do," he said, "that Hattie has no say in the matter. I'll see you in the morning."

"Sleep well," I murmured as he started up the stairs. I figured that he would probably go straight to bed and snore right through the twelve-o'clock appointment, and I was vastly relieved about it.

I stood in the front hall for a while, idly wondering what to do. Somehow I could not face lying in my room, sleepless and waiting for anything or nothing to happen.

I went slowly up the stairs after a while and came face to face with Detective Hatton, who was emerging from Hattie's room. He said, "Oh! I was looking for you."

I smiled innocently. "When did you arrive?"

"Came a few minutes ago," he said, showing signs of impatience. "Now what do you know about this robbery?"

I thought he looked tired and worried, and I decided to tell him all about the money. After all, he was the law and he ought to know what was going on. It developed that my appearance had diverted him from a visit to Ross, and Ross had said nothing previously, except that he had lost some money.

"I know all about that robbery," I said cheerfully. "I know who took the money and where it is now."

He very nearly groaned. "My good girl, why didn't you tell me before? I've been wasting valuable time over the thing."

"This is the first time I've seen you," I pointed out, "and I haven't your telephone number."

"Come, come, let's have it," he said, nearly dancing up and down.

I told him what I knew, and he considered it thoughtfully, his eyes staring into space.

"So you think it was money that Mrs. Barton found on the roof?"

"I can't be sure," I admitted, "but it seems very probable."

"The money that Mr. Ross Barton lost?"

I shrugged. "I suppose so. It isn't often that people go around the house hiding money."

"That's true. But if it was his, then who put it there?"

"Someone might have found it and stolen it and then hid it on the roof for safekeeping."

He said, "Maybe," and turned away from me and went and knocked on Ross's door. Watching him, I realized that I had forgotten to tell him about Hattie dropping the powder into Ross's coffee.

He knocked several times and then went in, but he was out again almost immediately. He passed me by without a word, which was a mistake, because I could have told him why it was impossible to rouse Ross.

He went back into Hattie's room and left the door open, so that I could see the crowd still milling around in there. He put them all out with very little ceremony and closed the door on Hattie and himself.

Mr. Keith deigned to notice me for the first time in several hours. "What are you doing here, Ellen? You should have retired to your room long ago."

He did not wait for me to think up an answer but took himself off to the third floor.

Oliver and Bill converged upon me, presumably for a little chat, but the chat developed into a disagreement with which I had nothing to do.

Oliver gave it as his opinion that a tramp was hiding somewhere about the place, emerging now and then to kill or rob, and if the police would only get busy they'd find him.

Bill took this amiss and declared with some heat that if Oliver could find so much as a pin that the police didn't know about Oliver could have Detective Hatton's place. Bill would recommend it.

"As for outside," Bill continued, still wounded, "there are no fewer than four cops hanging around. Just let you or anyone else try to get in or out without being seen."

I murmured, "Gracious! They must be getting wet."

Oliver went off to bed at that point. He said the only peace he got these days was in his dreams.

I asked Bill if he had found the animal.

He scratched his head and said, "Nope. I looked until I was staggerin', and then I took a nap on the sofa. Matter of fact, I don't believe there is an animal in the house."

"Oh yes," I said, "there's an animal all right. It's all ghost, except one of its paws. That one paw can be seen; the rest is spirit. It makes marks with that paw too. Next time you look don't bother hunting for a body, just look for a black paw."

Bill jerked his collar away from his neck and muttered feebly, "Listen, lady, pardon me, but I gotta go downstairs for a while."

He went off, and I sat down on the stairs because I had nothing else to do and nowhere to go. It was while I was sitting there that I had a brilliant thought. I decided that it must have been Franny who had stolen Ross's money.

CHAPTER THIRTY-ONE

I HAD SEEN Franny reaching out of that window on my arrival, and later, from the inside of the room, I had seen her again, doing the same thing. She must have hidden the money there, and Hattie must have known that she had stolen it, which would explain Hattie's frantic search of the top floor. It was probably known that Franny spent a lot of time on the top floor—and particularly among Alice's things—and Hattie would figure it as a likely spot to search. She had been rewarded too. It must have been money that she tucked into her dress, since she had had none before that time and plenty afterward.

I could hear Hattie's voice, loud and strident, behind her dosed door, and I pulled myself wearily off the stairs and laid my ear against the keyhole as delicately as Mr. Keith would have done it.

Detective Hatton seemed to have made progress, for Hattie was saying in an agitated voice, "That money doesn't belong to anyone else. It's mine—I found it. It must have been there for ages, because it was all wet and everything. I don't see why you think it belongs to that big-mouthed Ross. He told you he didn't put his money there."

Detective Hatton said, "Hush! Lower your voice! I don't want the whole house to know. Now tell me what you were doing when you happened to run across the money."

There was a dead silence which must have lasted fully a minute before Hattie burst out again: "You say you know who took that money. It's mine—and I don't care who took it—I want it back."

"Time enough for that," Detective Hatton said impatiently. "Right now I want to know what took you to the fourth floor when you found it."

There was another silence, and then Hattie said sullenly, "I just went up there to see if everything was all right."

"You were so concerned, in fact, that you practically tore the room of the deceased sister to shreds."

"I did no such thing," Hattie lied.

"Are you telling me that you left the room as you found it?"

Silence again. Then, "Well—not exactly. I may have left it a little untidy, but I certainly didn't tear it apart."

"Why should you have left it a little untidy?"

"I wanted to look in the other room. I was going to tidy up when I came back."

"So you went into the other room and looked there?" Hattie said, "Yes," and I thought she sounded a bit scared.

"For what were you looking?" Detective Hatton asked smoothly.

Hattie said, "Nothing," defiantly.

"I'm afraid I don't understand," Detective Hatton said, making it clear that he did. "Why did you make the room untidy if you were not looking for anything?"

"I didn't," Hattie shrieked. "I simply looked about to see if everything was still there. I did it for George. It always meant so much to him to keep those things nice."

Detective Hatton hushed her again and tried another tack. "Why did you go to the window and feel around outside?"

"I wanted to see if Franny had left anything out in the rain," Hattie said wildly. "She was always fussing around outside that window."

"Oh," said Detective Hatton, "I see. Thank you, Mrs. Barton."

I heard him making for the door, so I fled. I went back, climbed up to the fourth stair and flattened myself against the wall.

The detective closed Hattie's door and went along to Allan's room. He reappeared again very shortly and signaled to Bill, who had just come up the stairs.

Bill came along in a hurry and received a mild reproof. "Can't you keep those two men from getting drunk? They're both dead to the world, and I can't question them. It holds me up."

"I'm sorry, boss," Bill said. "I'll see if I can get 'em on their feet."

The detective shook his head. "No use now. I couldn't get anything intelligent out of them. You shouldn't have let them get that way in the first place."

"I'm sorry," Bill said again and scratched his head. "I told them to lay off, but they wouldn't."

I thought of Bill spending the entire afternoon on the fourth floor and sleeping through most of it and shook my head over his lies.

Detective Hatton said that he had something to think out and ordered Bill to accompany him to the kitchen and make coffee. They went off, and I had almost decided to go on upstairs when Hattie's door opened quietly. I watched her peer up and down the hall, and then she slipped quietly along to Ross's room and disappeared inside.

I remembered that Ross's room connected with Franny's by a bathroom, so I made my way there with all possible speed. The bathroom was in darkness and the door to Ross's room slightly open, so that I had a ringside seat.

Hattie was carefully searching through Ross's things by the dim glow of a night light.

I was a little puzzled. For what was she searching, if not the money? And how could it be the money, since she had discovered its loss only after she had dropped the powder into Ross's coffee? I remembered the emerald ring of which she had spoken to Allan and wondered whether that was what she was after. But why should she suppose it would be among Ross's things?

And certainly it seemed a bit exaggerated to give him a sleeping powder to facilitate her search for a ring.

She had nearly finished going through the bureau when Ross spoke.

He said, "Listen, sweetheart. If you want any one of my humble possessions I'd prefer that you ask for it. I only hope it's nothing in the clothing line, because your hip measurements are a bit more so than mine."

Hattie flung around with her mouth gaping. When she had recovered her breath she whispered harshly, "What are you doing awake?"

"Surprises you, doesn't it?" asked Ross comfortably. "But I assure you that it takes more than a dose of talcum powder to put me out."

"What do you mean? I don't know what you're talking about?" Hattie protested, making a very poor job of pretending innocence.

Ross said, "Oh, don't be a cluck. What are you looking for?"

"An emerald ring," Hattie replied promptly. "George always said it was to be mine, and I can't find it anywhere."

It was too pat, and I was convinced that if there ever had been an emerald ring Hattie knew very well what had become of it. She was after something else, something much more vital to her peace of mind.

However, she stuck to the ring explanation, and all Ross's sarcasm could not budge her. She finally admitted to having given him a powder, but she insisted that it was only a mild sedative—something George had taken to make him sleep.

"Sure, he took them," Ross agreed, "only he never knew it. You slipped them to him when you wanted to go out."

She denied that rather indifferently, and Ross presently let her go with a warning. "If I catch you mucking into my affairs again you'll be damned sorry."

Hattie departed in guilty haste, and I backed out of the bathroom and sped through Franny's silent, empty bedroom with little shivers creeping up and down my spine.

I made my way to the third floor and met Mr. Keith heading for the bathroom. I stopped him with brazen courage and asked, "Mr. Keith, who can shoot the straightest in this house?"

He froze over. "Mr. Allan is our best shot. And I shall personally see to it that he shoots you straight out of this house first thing in the morning."

I said, "Why, Mr. Keith! Your dignity! And if our Mr. Allan is the best shot around here he probably bumped off his sister Franny, because that job was done by an expert marksman."

His expression changed, and he looked a bit disconcerted and more than a little angry. "That is both silly and insulting to Mr. Allan," he said coldly. "Mr. Ross and Oliver are both expert marksmen, and if I do say so, I, myself—Why, when I was a boy in Scotland—"

I did not want to be conducted on a tour through his youth, so I said hastily, "All right, I believe you. Guess I'll go to bed now. Good night."

He said stiffly, "It is about time. Good night," and went on to the bathroom.

I watched him from behind my door while he filled the tub with water. Once Jennie opened the door of their room, just a crack, so that the world might not see her in her nightgown, and called, "When are you coming to bed?"

"Go yourself, my dear," he replied. "I shall be there in a minute."

Jennie retired and closed the door, and Mr. Keith came out of the bathroom and went quietly up the stairs to the fourth floor. Curiosity instantly became as a hair shirt to me, and I was goaded into following.

Mr. Keith was in the front room when I reached the upper hall, and he was making a peculiar chirping noise with his tongue.

My hair began to creep all over my head, and then he said suddenly and clearly, "Here, Alice. Here, Alice," and I got it.

It was the cat, of course. Evidently he knew about it and was trying to catch it, and I had a cold conviction that his intention was to drown it in the bathtub once he got his hands on it.

I understood about that cat at last. It must have belonged to Franny, who had named it Alice. Probably the window had been left open so that the creature could get air and exercise on the roof.

I hoped that Mr. Keith would not find the poor thing and went back to my room, accompanied by a chilling picture of him lowering a wriggling body into the cold water of the tub. I was afraid to do anything about it for fear of getting into trouble, and I hoped again, fervently; that the poor animal would be able to get away.

I left the door of my room open, so that I would know what was happening, and suddenly, before my eyes, a black cat scampered across the hall and down the stairs. It was a sooty black, with no light markings, and I understood why it had been so hard to find.

I went down the stairs after it, with some sort of vague idea that I could let it out, and then, perhaps, it might find a home somewhere else.

I caught another glimpse of it when I got to the second floor. It was streaking down the stairs to the front hall. I followed as fast as I could, but when I reached the hall it had disappeared. I opened the front door to give it free passage, in case it showed up again, and stood there for a moment, breathing the cool, wet air.

The veranda was brightly lighted, and I supposed it was so that the outlying policemen could clearly see arrivals and departures.

Part of the graveled walk was illuminated, and I noticed idly that someone's footsteps had dug deeply into the wet, spongy surface. Footsteps coming in. And there were none going out.

Those were Mr. Evans' footprints, and he had never gone out again. He had come into the house and disappeared into thin air.

CHAPTER THIRTY-TWO

I FORGOT all about the cat and could think only of Mr. Evans lying with horrible stillness in some obscure corner of the house. I closed the door and hurried back to the kitchen.

Detective Hatton and Bill were there. The detective was seated at the table, doing his thinking with the aid of several small piles of written notes, and Bill was juggling three oranges at once.

They looked up at me, and Bill said, "News—or maybe only gossip."

I told them about the footprints, and they made a rush for the front door. I followed and asked Detective Hatton, "Didn't you come in after Mr. Evans though?"

"I don't know," he said over his shoulder. "It doesn't matter, in any case, because I came in the back door. It was nearest to where I had parked my car."

They went out the front door and down the steps, and Bill produced a flashlight. They examined the footprints carefully, and I heard Bill say in a voice of surprise, "She's right."

I was shivering again, so I went back into the house. I did not want to see Mr. Evans when they found him, so I went straight up to my room, turned on the light and shut the door. I stretched out on the bed and lit a cigarette, but I could not stop shivering.

I was just beginning to relax a little, when something black and furry leaped onto the end of the bed.

I had let out a startled cry before I realized that it was the cat again. It arched its back and spat at me, and with my hands and voice both trembling, I began to try and make friends with it.

It was pretty wild, but after some patient effort I enticed it to a point where it allowed me to stroke its head and back. It wore a leather collar with a metal plate on which the word "Alice" was inscribed. I was fingering the plate curiously, when I noticed a small wad of paper wedged in between the metal and the leather. I worked it out, while the cat mewed plaintively, and while half my mind was concerned with the paper the other half nagged at me to get the poor creature some milk.

The paper proved to be a note, and it showed Franny up as a blackmailer of a mild sort. It read, "Dear Mr. Evans: I know that you cannot help looking at me frequently. Please don't be afraid to speak to me. I am interested in you too. Would like to meet you in town sometime for a cup of tea and a cozy chat. Yours? Hattie Barton. P.S. Am sending this by Franny—she's safe as houses, so send reply back by her. H. B."

I laughed a little and reflected that poor Hattie was ready for any man, as long as it meant a bit of excitement. And Franny had not been as safe as Hattie had carelessly supposed. Of course Franny would be highly suspicious of any note passing from Hattie to Mr. Evans, and she had probably opened it with a grim idea of saving the family honor in case it stood in peril. She must have congratulated herself on her foresight, after she had read it, and had blackmailed Hattie by threatening to show it to George. It was quite clear now Hattie's reason for going through the top floor so frantically. I decided, too, that she must have had some reason to think that Ross had got hold of the note.

I put the paper carefully away and went downstairs to get the cat some milk, after first closing my door so that it could not get out while I was gone.

I met Ross on the second floor. "What's going on downstairs?" he asked. "It's keeping me awake."

I explained about Mr. Evans.

"My God!" Ross exclaimed. "The poor old buzzard! This is terrible! We'll have to do something."

I began to shiver again and wished desperately that I was miles away from that house where some ghastly creature crept around doing dreadful things.

"I'll go and help," Ross said abruptly. He started down the stairs, and I followed and told him about the note I had found on the cat.

He never could be serious for very long, and he started to laugh. "No wonder the silly diz searched my room," he said at last.

"What do you mean?"

"I made a remark to her lately—something about how she ought to have another try at Mr. Evans, because you never knew about the saintly kind; sometimes they could sin as well or better than the next.

"She picked out the word 'another' and got all excited over it. I merely assumed that she had already had a go at him, but she must have thought that I had got hold of the note. Hence the business of poor old George's sleeping powder. The old coot never did sleep well."

We went on downstairs and came upon Detective Hatton and Bill in the back hall. They were pulling Mr. Evans out of the cupboard under the stairs.

I backed away, feeling sick and frightened. I didn't want to see anything, and I went and sat on the front stairs with my hands folded in my lap and my eyes staring into space.

Ross came and found me after a while and said kindly, "It's all right; he's not dead. Just a crack on the head, and he seems to be coming out of it. We've sent for the doctor."

They had put Mr. Evans on a couch in the sitting room, and I went along to have a look at him, feeling vastly relieved.

Detective Hatton was talking to him, although the poor man seemed to be barely conscious. But the detective kept repeating monotonously, "Who was it? Who hit you?"

Mr. Evans moaned and moved restlessly. After a while he said feebly, "I don't know—I was hit from behind. I don't know at all."

I went back to the front hall and thought feverishly, "Of course he doesn't know. Nobody ever saw this creeping horror—nobody ever will."

I glanced at the door of the sitting room. It was just a step from there to the hall closet. Easy to hit Mr. Evans from behind, and the work of a moment to drag him to the closet and hide him there.

Mr. Evans had come to see Allan on a matter of importance, and there had been an attempt to dispose of him. I widened my eyes, and suddenly I was running up the stairs, determined to try and rouse Allan. He might still be dead to the world, but he was capable of sobering up quickly, as I well knew.

I remembered the cat briefly and reminded myself to get her some milk when I had a breathing spell.

I knocked on Allan's door, and to my surprise, he opened it himself. He appeared to be quite sober.

He said, "All right, come in and tell me. I never saw such a nose for gossip in all my life."

"I thought you were drunk," I said suspiciously.

"I thought so too," he replied equably. "I've been working on it. I had a cold shower, for one thing."

"You weren't just pretending to be drunk?"

"No," he said flatly, "I was not. What did you want to tell me?"

I explained about Mr. Evans and asked anxiously, "You never did see him, did you?"

"No. I was a bit annoyed with him, anyway. He'd made an appointment with me for tomorrow morning, and just before dinner he must needs call up and change it to tonight, which didn't particularly suit me."

"I'll bet it didn't," I murmured, squinting at him. "It's too bad he didn't leave it for tomorrow. But I think you ought to go down. He's conscious and maybe he can deliver his important message to you."

He said, "Yes," with his eyes on my face, and he didn't seem to be thinking of Mr. Evans. "You stay here," he added.

"I'm not staying anywhere in this house alone if I can hobble on one leg to where there's company."

"Don't be a coward," he said mildly. "I'm afraid you're too fond of company. You probably wouldn't like living in this house."

I stared at him, and he stared back.

"What do you mean?" I asked, trying to sound mad.

"What I say. You probably wouldn't care for it. Unless you interested yourself in something—golf, perhaps."

"Are you intimating—?"

He kissed me without bothering to ask my permission. "I know you'd marry me, were I to ask you, sis. Of course there's one thing—you kiss like a veteran."

"Thanks for the diploma," I said shortly and walked out of the room, no longer trying to be mad, because I was genuinely furious.

He followed close behind me, and when we neared the sitting room he said with a hint of laughter, "Don't trip and spoil the whole thing."

I couldn't think up anything good enough for that, so I entered the sitting room in silence.

The doctor had not yet arrived, and Mr. Evans was moaning a little. Detective Hatton sat beside him, gloomy and silent, and Bill stood in front of the fireplace, chewing on a straw that appeared to have come from one of Jennie's best brooms. Ross had disappeared.

Allan and the detective exchanged greetings, and Allan said, "He had a message for me. Any hope of getting it from him now?"

The detective shrugged. "No harm trying. Go ahead."

Allan leaned over the couch and asked in a low, clear voice, "Have you something important to tell me, Mr. Evans?"

Mr. Evans groaned, moved his head restlessly and opened his eyes. "Oh. Mr. Barton. Yes, it was Miss Franny. She said I was to see you if anything happened to her. She phoned me, you know—asked me to come to her—said she wanted to tell me something."

"Yes, I know," Allan said with faint impatience.

"She said if anything happened to her before I saw her I must remind you of a remark she had made to you previously. 'The outer appearance of honesty is not a guarantee of inner honesty.'"

Allan straightened up, looked puzzled and still faintly impatient. "She was always saying things like that. But I'll give it some headwork and see if I can hit onto a connection."

The doctor arrived just then, and after a brief examination decided that Mr. Evans could be moved to his home. He was carried away, and Detective Hatton and Bill went along with him.

Allan went upstairs, apparently to do his headwork, and since dignity forbade me to follow him I remained in the hall.

The door of the closet from which Mr. Evans had been rescued was still open, and I walked slowly over, with my spine creeping, and looked inside. The place was cluttered with dusty rubbers, old umbrellas and an odd assortment of coats. I stared at the mess rather blankly, and then I remembered about Ross's hiding place for his reserve money. I stepped in and looked around for a break in the plaster. I found it without any trouble, deep in the corner and rather high up. The plaster had crumbled and left a neat little hole.

I inserted my hand and drew out a small, heavy cardboard box and a piece of paper. The box contained bullets; the paper had a written list: "Lemons, sugar, potatoes, salt, water cress." And the handwriting was my own.

CHAPTER THIRTY-THREE

MEMORY STIRRED and suddenly flashed brightly. Jennie had ordered me to write the list while she went through the pantry and called out what was needed.

Other little things tumbled into place, and I stood there, shaking, with my heart in my mouth, as the picture took clear shape in my mind.

I ran to the front door and peered out, but there was no sign of Detective Hatton or Bill, and I completely forgot about the four policemen who were guarding the house.

Allan's twelve-o'clock appointment flashed into my mind, and I began to sweat with fear. The old-fashioned clock in the hall showed three minutes past twelve, which meant that Allan had almost certainly gone to the fourth floor to meet the writer of those notes. The notes had been written this morning, with Mr. Evans supposedly due the following morning, bearing a message of importance! Plenty of time to decoy Allan to the fourth floor and get rid of him before morning!

I didn't wait for anything more; I flew all the way up to the fourth floor with my heart pounding in my throat. I took the last flight swiftly but quietly and hesitated on the top step. It was black dark and as silent as the grave.

I crept toward the front room where the meeting was due to take place. As I neared the door I heard the sound of low voices, and I cautiously edged my head around the jamb and looked in. Allan and Mr. Keith were conversing in whispers, their faces weirdly lighted by a flickering candle in a heavy brass candlestick that Mr. Keith held above their heads.

I held my breath and heard Mr. Keith say, "I'll put the candle out, sir, and we'll wait for him in the dark. This candlestick will be an effective weapon."

Allan said, "All right, but you'll have to keep very quiet."

Mr. Keith extinguished the candle, and I slipped into the room and made straight for the spot where the glow had flickered out.

I was barely in time. Mr. Keith, with the heavy candlestick clutched in his hands, had both arms high in the air over Allan's head.

I pushed wildly, and Mr. Keith went crashing to the floor.

CHAPTER THIRTY-FOUR

Mr. Keith, stripped of his dignity, sat in the sitting room, alternately scowling and cringing. Everyone was there except Jennie, who had been put to bed by the doctor. She had announced that she did not believe it and never would.

Mr. Keith refused to say anything for a while, until Detective Hatton bolstered up his vanity. "We can convict you, Keith, but your crimes are so clever and unusual that I should take a scientific interest in hearing your story."

Mr. Keith lost his scowl, straightened up and smoothed back his hair. He gazed at the ceiling and began with a hint of his old dignity: "It was all a simply incredible fuss that was made over a mere three hundred dollars.

"I have always been honest and greatly respected in the church. But if I find anything around the house that apparently does not belong to anyone I see no reason why it should not belong to me.

"I was cleaning out that closet under the stairs, when I discovered the hole in the plaster, and thought I might repair it myself. Thus I found the three hundred dollars. Mr. George happened into the hall at that moment and, stopping to look in, saw me with the money in my hands.

"He said, 'Put it back, Keith, it belongs to Mr. Ross.'

"I said, 'Yes sir,' and put it back. But I thought it over later, and I reasoned that it belonged as much to me as to anyone. I took it and hid it again, wedged under a shingle outside the dormer window in the front room on the fourth floor.

"Two days later Mr. George came to me and said that the money was missing. He ordered me to put it back and added that I was to confess my sin to the parson of our church, Mr. Evans.

"Mr. Evans is a fine and upright gentleman, and I have always been proud of his high opinion of me and of my unique standing in his church. I am an elder. I could not go to him with such a story. I refused and denied having taken the money, but Mr. George would not believe me.

"He set a deadline—the fourteenth—and circled that date on all the calendars in the house. He warned me that if I failed to conform he would take the whole thing to Mr. Evans himself. In the intervening time he sat at the dining-room table each night until twelve o'clock, waiting for me to come to him and submit.

"I could not do it. I would not confess to a sin when I felt that no sin had been committed. I did bring the money to Mr. George with a story that I had found it in the coal bin, but he would have none of it. I had transgressed, he said, and I must confess and set it right.

"I went to church the night I killed him, and Mr. Evans gave a very fine sermon. I made up my mind then that I could not give up my position in the church; it was a monstrous injustice.

"When I got home Mr. George was sitting in the dining room; all the calendars were marked with my last day of grace, and I was possessed by hot, righteous anger. Mr. George had no right to set himself up as judge, and I determined that he was not going to ruin my life.

"After Jennie had gone to sleep I slipped the string off my toe and went back downstairs. I used the front stairs and went into the sitting room. Just then I heard someone come down the back stairs and walk along the hall to the front. It was the new maid, and I saw her go into the drawing room.

"I was distressed, but what I had to do must be done that night, since it was Mr. George's deadline. I got the gun out of the drawer and ascertained that it was loaded, and then I heard someone coming down the front stairs. This time it was Mr. Allan, and he, also, went into the drawing room.

"I knew that I must get my job done quickly, for I was in a precarious position. But the gun had a silencer, and I hoped to get back upstairs without being noticed.

"I went into the dining room, and Mr. George smiled at me, thinking he had won. I walked close to him and shot him dead.

"I thought I might need the gun again, so I hid it and both boxes of bullets in the woodpile. One of the boxes had only one bullet left, and after I had loaded that bullet into the gun I thoughtlessly hid the empty box with the other one in my agitation.

"I thought I was quite safe, but Miss Franny began to bother me, and I was horrified by the realization that Mr. George might have told her all about it. I tore all the calendars off, hoping that she had not noticed. But I was her friend. I cared for her cat, fed it and saw that her possession of it was kept secret from the others.

"We kept the animal in the top front room, and it went out onto the roof for air and exercise. Miss Franny worried a great deal for fear it would fall off and insisted on keeping the window open, so that it could get back inside.

"On the night I killed Mr. George, Miss Franny had left the front-room door open, and the cat escaped into the house. She was frantic and spent most of her time searching for the creature, but as far I know, it has not been found since. After Miss Franny was laid away I determined to drown the beast in the bathtub, but I never caught up with it.

"I did not worry too much until at the inquest Miss Hattie announced that Mr. George had told Miss Franny everything. I gave it more thought after that and regretfully decided that Miss Franny must go.

"It was difficult to get at her, for she took to spending her nights in Ellen's room. And then I overheard her speaking to Mr. Evans on the telephone, making an appointment and telling him that she had decided to confide in him. She went on to say that if anything happened to her first Mr. Evans must remind Mr. Allan that an appearance of honesty did not prove a person honest.

"I did not think Mr. Allan would make anything out of that, but I knew Miss Franny must go before the morning.

"Jennie did not sleep well that night, and it was fairly late before I could get out. I got the gun from the woodpile; I had it and the bullets in a hollowed log, so that they were not discovered when the pile was searched.

"I went upstairs and waited just inside my door. I was hoping that she would come out and go up to look for the cat, but she did not appear. Finally I could wait no longer, and I crept to Ellen's door. I could hear Miss Franny rocking, and I carefully pushed the door wider and shot several times. I am a good marksman.

"I was back in bed, with my toe in the string, before the disturbance awoke Jennie. I had pushed the gun down to the bottom of the bed, under the bedclothes, and there I left it until I was sent downstairs, when I took it with me and replaced it in the woodpile.

"Later I was very disturbed about having walked straight to the woodpile in my sleep. I feared that I might reveal myself, so I removed the gun and box of bullets. I hid the bullets in the closet in the hole where I had found the money, but the gun would not fit. I was pressed for time, so I put it in the washroom under the telephone book for the time being. After that I made Ellen help me search the woodpile. She found the empty box that I must have dropped there, and Jennie found the gun. I felt that it did not matter much, since I hardly expected to need the gun again.

"Then today Mr. Evans phoned Mr. Allan and made an appointment for tomorrow morning. I knew he was going to deliver Miss Franny's message, and I began to worry. Perhaps I had been too confident, and the message would have some special significance for Mr. Allan that would involve me. I felt trapped and surrounded, and I made up my mind to fight my way out.

"Mr. Allan would have to go, but I wanted to avoid hurting Mr. Evans if at all possible.

"I did not know what to do about Mr. Allan. I no longer had the gun, and I could not think of anything, until I happened to see that grocery list that Ellen had written when I was emptying the wastebasket.

"I knew that Ellen was not a regular maid. Mrs. Allan Barton had spoken to her by telephone twice. Bill told me that she was seeing Mr. Allan secretly, and I came to the conclusion that they were lovers.

"I copied Ellen's handwriting carefully and wrote two notes to Mr. Allan. I hardly expected the forgery to deceive Mr. Allan, but I figured correctly that he would keep the rendezvous.

"I did not know that Mr. Evans had changed appointment, and when he came here tonight I was stunned. I put him into the sitting room and went up to Mr. Allan, and there I had a stroke of luck. Mr. Allan was drunk and sleeping, so I left him and came down again. I knew he would not remember that I had made no effort to rouse him.

"Ellen and Mr. Ross had disappeared from the back hall, and when I returned to the sitting room Mr. Evans was seated with his back to me. The brass candlestick was on a table beside me, and I hit him with it and put him into the closet. I hated doing it, for he is my ideal of what a man should be. I am very glad that he was not seriously injured.

"I went straight to the kitchen and made some remark about Mr. Allan, and I believe Jennie went and tried to get him up.

"I had left the candlestick in the sitting room, since it was not stained, and I had wiped it carefully, but it gave me an idea. I knew there was another such candlestick in one of the storage rooms, and I took it out and placed it in that front room. I was prepared with a candle and matches in my pocket, and I proceeded to remove the electric fuses on the top floor. All this, of course, after Jennie was asleep.

"I met Mr. Allan at the head of the stairs, explained that there was some trouble with the lights and told him in whispers that I had seen Oliver creeping up here some time before. It should have worked, and would have, but for this girl—this painted, godless creature. Had she not come, I should still have Mr. Evans' friendship and the three hundred dollars that is rightfully mine.

"The two who died deserved to go for their cruel interference, and it is a pity about the one who was saved. A coarse, immoral man, recently divorced, and already looking for another victim."

CHAPTER THIRTY-FIVE

MR. KEITH was removed, and the law went with him.

Oliver gave us a cheery good night and left with the observation that he thought he might catch some sleep now. Hattie said she thought she'd go, too, and could be heard hurrying up the back stairs after him.

I stood up and said coldly, "I think I'll go to bed myself."

Allan grinned at me. "Wait a minute. Did you know it was Keith when you came flying up the stairs and saved my life?"

"I knew it was Keith when I found that grocery list I had written," I said soberly. "Anyone in the kitchen could have known I'd written it, but

Mr. Keith had been filling up the tub in order to drown the cat, and since he knew of its existence he must have been the one who was helping Franny to care for it. She needed someone to help her if she was to keep it a secret. Therefore, I figured she was speaking of Mr. Keith when she said that one good turn deserved another and refused to identify the person of whom she was afraid. Also, he was privileged to use the front stairs, and someone had come down the front stairs after you on the night George was killed."

"How about that Bible?" Ross asked.

"Franny probably had a fit when she saw what the cat had done to it," Allan said. "I suppose she wanted to get it repaired on the quiet and as quickly as possible. She took it down to Callie's room, I expect, with the intention of carting it off as soon as she had a chance."

"I wonder who took it up again," I said thoughtfully.

"Keith," Allan replied. "He didn't want it noticed in your room or anywhere else. If it were found out that there was a cat in the house it might also be discovered that he had been taking care of it. And it was obvious that Franny had been protecting someone."

"Let's get it all swept up," I suggested, glancing doubtfully at Allan. "That little memorandum book of yours. It said, 'Must speak to George by the fourteenth.'"

Allan laughed. "Pure coincidence. Hattie had borrowed a fiver from Jennie, and Jennie came and told me about it. I object to that sort of thing, and I gave Hattie until the fourteenth to pay it back, when I was going to speak to George rather forcibly about it."

"Where is Hattie's emerald ring?" I asked.

"Only a coverup." Allan shrugged. "George gave her the ring long ago, and she pawned it pretty promptly. I think she was about to redeem it with that money of Ross's which she accidentally found on the roof, but—"

"But I got it back first," Ross interrupted, laughing. "It's downright vulgar, the moneygrubbing that goes on in this house. And Allan is able to sit and play boss, because he tripled his inheritance, while the rest of us lost or spent ours without delay."

I said, "He's stingy with it too."

"You mean because I offered Selma five dollars and fifty cents a week alimony?" Allan asked mildly. "My jokes always go over the heads of you girls."

I gasped and asked, "Did I have to go through all this because Selma is a dope and took you seriously?"

He laughed. "I burned the letters she was making such a fuss about, and I agreed to the alimony that she wanted. By way of return, I received a sweet letter, intimating that it would not be for long, since she has a rich beau."

I nodded. I knew about that rich beau, and although Selma had been pretending that he was not really interested in her she doesn't pretend very well.

"What did that message of old Evans mean to you?" Ross asked. "How was it important?"

"As it happens, I didn't get it quite straight," said Allan. "Franny and I were dining alone some weeks ago, and I remarked to her that the monthly bills seemed to be pretty high. She made that remark then about the appearance of honesty being misleading sometimes, and I remember that Keith was in the room at the time. I paid no attention to it—Franny was always saying things like that—but Keith must have known that she was referring to him. Tonight, when Evans relayed the message, I figured that it must mean one of the servants, and when I got to the top floor and saw Keith I supposed it was he, but he immediately put me off by telling me that he had seen Oliver creeping up there and had followed him. I decided that it must be Oliver at that point—which was pretty silly, because Oliver hasn't any outer appearance of honesty."

Ross yawned. "I'm going to bed, as the excitement seems to be over. By the way, Allan, what are you going to give our little Ellen for having saved your life?"

"After due thought," Allan said gravely, "I've decided to bestow my hand upon her. She can marry me any day, starting tomorrow."

"Good!" said Ross, yawning again. "That'll be a nice present for her."

I opened my mouth to hurl insults at both of them, but Allan spoke first.

"It's all right," he said; "you needn't thank me—it's nothing. Only remember, you'll have to take what comes with me, a vulgar cream-colored roadster and a mink coat."

"Oh," I said, cooling down rapidly. "That's different."

THE END

Rue Morgue Press Titles as of March 2001

Black Corridors by Constance & Gwenyth Little. Some people go to the beach for their vacations, others go to the mountains. Jessie Warren's Aunt Isabel preferred checking herself into the hospital where she thoroughly enjoyed a spot of bad health although the doctors were at a loss to spot any cause. As usual, Jessie and her sister tossed to see who would accompany Aunt Isabel to the hospital—and, as usual, Jessie lost. Jessie's mother pointed out that pampering her rich aunt might do her some good in the future, even if it means that Jessie has to miss a date or two with some promising beaux. Aunt Isabel insists on staying in her favorite room, which means the current patient has to be dispossessed. And when that man's black wallet turns up missing, just about everyone joins in the hunt. That's about the time someone decided to start killing blondes. For the first time in her life Jessie's glad to have her bright red hair, even if a certain doctor—who doesn't have the money or the looks of her other beaux—enjoys making fun of those flaming locks. But after Jessie stumbles across a couple of bodies and starts snooping around, the murderer figures the time has come to switch from blondes to redheads. First published in 1940, *Black Corridors* is Constance & Gwenyth Little at their wackiest best.   **0-915230-33-X $14.00**

The Black Stocking by Constance & Gwenyth Little. Irene Hastings, who can't decide which of her two fiancés she should marry, is looking forward to a nice vacation, and everything would have been just fine had not her mousy friend Ann asked to be dropped off at an insane asylum so she could visit her sister. When the sister escapes, just about everyone, including a handsome young doctor, mistakes Irene for the runaway loony, and she is put up at an isolated private hospital under house arrest, pending final identification. Only there's not a bed to be had in the hospital. One of the staff is already sleeping in a tent on the grounds, so it's decided that Irene is to share a bedroom with young Dr. Ross Munster, much to the consternation of both parties. On the other hand, Irene's much-married mother Elise, an Auntie Mame type who rushes to her rescue, figures that the young doctor has son-in-law written all over him. She also figures there's plenty of room in that bedroom for herself as well. In the meantime, Irene runs into a headless nurse, a corpse that won't stay put, an empty coffin, a missing will, and a mysterious black stocking. As Elise would say, "Mong Dew!" First published in 1946.   **0-915230-30-5 $14.00**

The Black-Headed Pins by Constance & Gwenyth Little. "...a zany, fun-loving puzzler spun by the sisters Little—it's celluloid screwball comedy printed on paper. The charm of this book lies in the lively banter between characters and the breakneck pace of the story."—Diane Plumley, *Dastardly Deeds*. "For a strong example of their work, try (this) very funny and inventive 1938 novel of a dysfunctional family Christmas." Jon L. Breen, *Ellery Queen's Mystery Magazine*.   **0-915230-25-9 $14.00**

The Black Gloves by Constance & Gwenyth Little. "I'm relishing every madcap moment."—*Murder Most Cozy*. Welcome to the Vickers estate near East Orange, New Jersey, where the middle class is destroying the neighborhood, erecting their horrid little cottages, playing on the Vickers tennis court, and generally disrupting the comfortable life of Hammond Vickers no end. Why does there also have to be a corpse in the cellar? First published in 1939.   **0-915230-20-8 $14.00**

The Black Honeymoon by Constance & Gwenyth Little. Can you murder someone with feathers? If you don't believe feathers are lethal, then you probably haven't read a Little mystery. No, Uncle Richard wasn't tickled to death—though we can't make the same guarantee for readers—but the hyper-allergic rich man did manage to sneeze himself into the hereafter. First published in 1944.   **0-915230-21-6 $14.00**

Great Black Kanba by Constance & Gwenyth Little. "If you love train mysteries as much as I do, hop on the Trans-Australia Railway in *Great Black Kanba*, a fast and funny 1944 novel by the talented (Littles)."—Jon L. Breen, *Ellery Queen's Mystery*

Magazine. "I have decided to add *Kanba* to my favorite mysteries of all time list!...a zany ride I'll definitely take again and again."—Diane Plumley in the Murder Ink newsletter. When a young American woman wakes up on an Australian train with a bump on her head and no memory, she suddenly finds out that she's engaged to two different men and the chief suspect in a murder case. It all adds up to some delightful mischief—call it Cornell Woolrich on laughing gas. **0-915230-22-4 $14.00**

The Grey Mist Murders by Constance & Gwenyth Little. Who—or what—is the mysterious figure that emerges from the grey mist to strike down several passengers on the final leg of a round-the-world sea voyage? Is it the same shadowy entity that persists in leaving three matches outside Lady Marsh's cabin every morning? And why does one flimsy negligee seem to pop up at every turn? When Carla Bray first heard things go bump in the night, she hardly expected to find a corpse in the adjoining cabin. Nor did she expect to find herself the chief suspect in the murders. This 1938 effort was the Littles' first book. **0-915230-26-7 $14.00**

Brief Candles by Manning Coles. From Topper to Aunt Dimity, mystery readers have embraced the cozy ghost story. Four of the best were written by Manning Coles, the creator of the witty Tommy Hambledon spy novels. First published in 1954, *Brief Candles* is likely to produce more laughs than chills as a young couple vacationing in France run into two gentlemen with decidedly old-world manners. What they don't know is that James and Charles Latimer are ancestors of theirs who shuffled off this mortal coil some 80 years earlier when, emboldened by strong drink and with only a pet monkey and an aged waiter as allies, the two made a valiant, foolish and quite fatal attempt to halt a German advance during the Franco-Prussian War of 1870. Now these two ectoplasmic gentlemen and their spectral pet monkey Ulysses have been summoned from their unmarked graves because their visiting relatives are in serious trouble. But before they can solve the younger Latimers' problems, the three benevolent spirits light brief candles of insanity for a tipsy policeman, a recalcitrant banker, a convocation of English ghostbusters, and a card-playing rogue who's wanted for murder. "As felicitously foolish as a collaboration of (P.G.) Wodehouse and Thorne Smith."—Anthony Boucher. "For those who like something out of the ordinary. Lighthearted, very funny.'—*The Sunday Times*. "A gay, most readable story."—*The Daily Telegraph* **0-915230-24-0 $14.00**

Happy Returns by Manning Coles. The ghostly Latimers and their pet spectral monkey Ulysses return from the grave when Uncle Quentin finds himself in need of their help—it seems the old boy is being pursued by an old flame who won't take no for an answer in her quest to get him to the altar. Along the way, our courteous and honest spooks thwart a couple of bank robbers, unleash a bevy of circus animals on an unsuspecting French town, help out the odd person or two and even "solve" a murder—with the help of the victim. The laughs start practically from the first page and don't stop until Ulysses slides down the bannister, glass of wine in hand, to drink a toast to returning old friends. **0-915230-31-3 $14.00**

The Chinese Chop by Juanita Sheridan. The postwar housing crunch finds Janice Cameron, newly arrived in New York City from Hawaii, without a place to live until she answers an ad for a roommate. It turns out the advertiser is an acquaintance from Hawaii, Lily Wu, whom critic Anthony Boucher (for whom Bouchercon, the World Mystery Convention, is named) described as "the exquisitely blended product of Eastern and Western cultures" and the only female sleuth that he "was devotedly in love with," citing "that odd mixture of respect for her professional skills and delight in her personal charms." First published in 1949, this ground-breaking book was the first of four to feature Lily and be told by her Watson, Janice, a first-time novelist. No sooner do Lily and Janice move into a rooming house in Washington Square than a corpse is found in the basement. In Lily Wu, Sheridan created one of the most believable—and memorable—female sleuths of her day. **0-915230-32-1 $14.00**

Death on Milestone Buttress by Glyn Carr. Abercrombie ("Filthy") Lewker was looking forward to a fortnight of climbing in Wales after a grueling season touring England with his Shakespearean company. Young Hilary Bourne thought the holiday would be a pleasant change from her dreary job at the bank, as well as a chance to renew her acquaintance with a certain young scientist. Neither one expected this bucolic outing to turn deadly but when one of their party is killed during what should have been an easy climb on the Milestone Buttress, Filthy and Hilary turn detective. Nearly every member of the climbing party had reason to hate the victim but each one also had an alibi for the time of the murder. Filthy and Hilary retrace the route of the fatal climb before returning to their lodgings where, in the grand tradition of Nero Wolfe, Filthy confronts the suspects and points his finger at the only person who could have committed the crime. Filled with climbing details sure to appeal to both expert climbers and armchair mountaineers alike, *Death on Milestone Buttress* was published in England in 1951, the first of fifteen detective novels in which Lewker outwitted murderers on peaks scattered around the globe, from Wales to Switzerland to the Himalayas. **0-915230-29-1 $14.00**

Murder is a Collector's Item by Elizabeth Dean. "(It) froths over with the same effervescent humor as the best Hepburn-Grant films."—Sujata Massey. "Completely enjoyable."—*New York Times*. "Fast and funny."—*The New Yorker*. Twenty-six-year-old Emma Marsh isn't much at spelling or geography and perhaps she butchers the odd literary quotation or two, but she's a keen judge of character and more than able to hold her own when it comes to selling antiques or solving murders. Originally published in 1939, *Murder is a Collector's Item* was the first of three books featuring Emma. Smoothly written and sparkling with dry, sophisticated humor, this milestone combines an intriguing puzzle with an entertaining portrait of a self-possessed young woman on her own at the end of the Great Depression. **0-915230-19-4 $14.00**

Murder is a Serious Business by Elizabeth Dean. It's 1940 and the Thirsty Thirties are over but you couldn't tell it by the gang at J. Graham Antiques, where clerk Emma Marsh, her would-be criminologist boyfriend Hank, and boss Jeff Graham trade barbs in between shots of scotch when they aren't bothered by the rare customer. Trouble starts when Emma and crew head for a weekend at Amos Currier's country estate to inventory the man's antiques collection. It isn't long before the bodies start falling and once again Emma is forced to turn sleuth in order to prove that her boss isn't a killer. "Judging from (this book) it's too bad she didn't write a few more."—Mary Ann Steel, *I Love a Mystery*. **0-915230-28-3 $14.95**

Murder, Chop Chop by James Norman. "The book has the butter-wouldn't-melt-in-his-mouth cool of Rick in *Casablanca*."—*The Rocky Mountain News*. "Amuses the reader no end."—*Mystery News*. "This long out-of-print masterpiece is intricately plotted, full of eccentric characters and very humorous indeed. Highly recommended."—*Mysteries by Mail*. Meet Gimiendo Hernandez Quinto, a gigantic Mexican who once rode with Pancho Villa and who now trains *guerrilleros* for the Nationalist Chinese government when he isn't solving murders. At his side is a beautiful Eurasian known as Mountain of Virtue, a woman as dangerous to men as she is irresistible. Together they look into the murder of Abe Harrow, an ambulance driver who appears to have died at three different times. There's also a cipher or two to crack, a train with a mind of its own, and Chiang Kai-shek's false teeth, which have gone mysteriously missing. First published in 1942. **0-915230-16-X $13.00**

Death at The Dog by Joanna Cannan. "Worthy of being discussed in the same breath with an Agatha Christie or Josephine Tey...anyone who enjoys Golden Age mysteries will surely enjoy this one."—Sally Fellows, *Mystery News*. "Skilled writing and brilliant characterization."—*Times of London*. "An excellent English rural tale."—Jacques Barzun & Wendell Hertig Taylor in *A Catalogue of Crime*. Set in late 1939 during the first anxious months of World War II, *Death at The Dog*, first published in 1941, is a wonderful example of the classic English detective novel that flourished between the two World Wars. Set in a picturesque village filled with thatched-roof cottages, eccentric villagers and genial pubs, it's as well-plotted as a Christie, with clues abundantly and fairly planted, and as deftly written as the best of Sayers or Marsh, filled with quotable lines and perceptive observations on the human condition. **0-915230-23-2 14.00**

They Rang Up the Police by Joanna Cannan. "Just delightful."—*Sleuth of Baker Street* Pick-of-the-Month. "A brilliantly plotted mystery...splendid character study...don't miss this one, folks. It's a keeper."—Sally Fellows, *Mystery News*. When Delia Cathcart and Major Willoughby disappear from their quiet English village one morning in July 1937, it looks like a simple case of a frustrated spinster running off for a bit of fun with a straying husband. But as the hours turn into days, Inspector Guy Northeast begins to suspect that she may have been the victim of foul play. Never published in the United States, *They Rang Up the Police* appeared in England in 1939. **0-1915230-27-5 $14.00**

Cook Up a Crime by Charlotte Murray Russell. "Perhaps the mother of today's 'cozy' mystery . . . amateur sleuth Jane has a personality guaranteed to entertain the most demanding reader."—Andy Plonka, *The Mystery Reader*. "Some wonderful old time recipes...highly recommended."—*Mysteries by Mail*. Meet Jane Amanda Edwards, a self-styled "full-fashioned" spinster who complains she hasn't looked at herself in a full-length mirror since Helen Hokinson started drawing for *The New Yorker*. But you can always count on Jane to look into other people's affairs, especially when there's a juicy murder case to investigate. In this 1951 title Jane goes searching for recipes (included between chapters) for a cookbook project and finds a body instead. And once again her lily-of-the-field brother Arthur goes looking for love, finds strong drink, and is eventually discovered clutching the murder weapon. **0-915230-18-6 $13.00**

The Man from Tibet by Clyde B. Clason. Locked inside the Tibetan Room of his Chicago apartment, the rich antiquarian was overheard repeating a forbidden occult chant under the watchful eyes of Buddhist gods. When the doors were opened it appeared that he had succumbed to a heart attack. But the elderly Roman historian and sometime amateur sleuth Theocritus Lucius Westborough is convinced that Adam Merriweather's death was anything but natural and that the weapon was an eighth century Tibetan manuscript. If it's murder, who could have done it, and how? Suspects abound. There's Tsongpun Bonbo, the gentle Tibetan lama from whom the manuscript was originally stolen; Chang, Merriweather's scholarly Tibetan secretary who had fled a Himalayan monastery; Merriweather's son Vincent, who disliked his father and stood to inherit a fortune; Dr. Jed Merriweather, the dead man's brother, who came to Chicago to beg for funds to continue his archaeological digs in Asia; Dr. Walters, the dead man's physician, who guarded a secret; and Janice Shelton, his young ward, who found herself being pushed by Merriweather into marrying his son. How the murder was accomplished has earned praise from such impossible crime connoisseurs as Robert C.S. Adey, who cited Clason's "highly original and practical locked-room murder method." **0-915230-17-8 $14.00**

The Mirror by Marlys Millhiser. "Completely enjoyable."—*Library Journal*. "A great deal of fun."—*Publishers Weekly*. How could you not be intrigued by a novel in which "you find the main character marrying her own grandfather and giving birth to her own mother?" Such is the situation in this classic novel, originally published in 1978, of two women who end up living each other's lives. Twenty-year-old Shay Garrett is not aware that she's pregnant and is having second thoughts about marrying Marek Weir when she's suddenly transported back 78 years in time into the body of Brandy McCabe, her own grandmother, who is unwillingly about to be married off to miner Corbin Strock. Shay's in shock but she still recognizes that the picture of her grandfather that hangs in the family home doesn't resemble her husband-to-be. But marry Corbin she does and off she goes to the high mining town of Nederland, where this thoroughly modern young woman has to learn to cope with such things as wood cooking stoves and—to her—old-fashioned attitudes about sex. In the meantime, Brandy McCabe is finding it even harder to cope with life in the Boulder, Colorado, of 1978. **0-915230-15-1 $14.95**

About The Rue Morgue Press

The Rue Morgue Press vintage mystery line is designed to bring back into print those books that were favorites of readers between the turn of the century and the 1960s. The editors welcome suggestions for reprints. To receive our catalog or make suggestions, write The Rue Morgue Press, P.O. Box 4119, Boulder, Colorado 80306. (1-800-699-6214).